Jason St

INTO THE

FLAMES

Jason Summers

For Winnie

2/9/24

3.50

Chapter One

Standing in the old, rusted machinery shed, Arthur Smith
listened to the weather reporter on the wireless radio on his
timber workbench.

'Forecast today has now been revised to forty-one degrees,
three degrees higher than what we first reported earlier this
week. The NSW fire services have now changed the fire
danger warning from extreme to catastrophic in the
Menindee, Pooncarie, and Darfield regions. Anyone who is
still in these areas is being told to evacuate immediately.
100km/h winds are due in a north-westerly direction which
will prove fatal for anyone who plans on trying to stay and
save their homes.'

He turned the radio off and kept his right hand held on the
thick hose which ran from the large water tank in the back of
the shed, and onto his spray rig on his 4-wheel drive
motorbike.

Bloody arseholes. Who do they think they are? I've been farming this region for my whole life, like my father before me. Plus, we've never had a single bad bushfire in Darfield. The wind will change, it always does, he thought to himself.

Watching the water reach the top of the spray rig tank, he turned the old Honda pump off. Now, with the only noise in the shed being the idling of the old 4-wheel motorbike, he could hear the wind starting to pick up, with the pinging of loose leaves and gumnuts showering the shed roof.

Where the hell was Vanessa? His wife had headed into town with their son Joe to buy more hose from the farm supply store a few hours earlier. The old spray rig on the bike didn't have enough pressure to reach the high gutters of his childhood home and he hoped with the longer hose, he could attach it directly to the 100,000-litre steel tank he had had installed on the property five years earlier and fill his gutters with much-needed water in preparation, just in case all of this news on the TV and radio was actually right.

Looking out to the front gate, he saw the maroon Hilux ute make its way through the opening and down their long driveway at a much faster pace than usual. Skidding to a stop in a hail of dust and gravel, Arthur's wife, Vanessa, opened the door of the ute as it was still coming to a stop. With a panic-stricken look at her husband, she yelled in his direction.

'Arthur! Why haven't you answered your mobile? I've been trying to call you all morning?!'

He cursed himself silently. He had only had a mobile phone for a month and had left it on the passenger seat of his ute. He really needed to start remembering to keep it on him.

'Sorry darl, I left it in my ute.'

'Have you seen Belle?! Is she inside the house?'

He thought back to his morning and tried to remember if he saw Belle, his seventeen-year-old daughter, getting ready for school.

'I'm not sure, love. I headed out early to give John a hand. His tractor was playi..'

Vanessa cut over the top of him. 'Jesus Christ, Arthur, half this town is about to go up in the flames and you haven't seen her?'

He hadn't seen his wife in a panic like this in a long time. As he felt her stress levels rising, he too began to worry about the whereabouts of his daughter.

'Have you tried Anna's? She might have shacked up there. Let's head up to the house and I'll grab my phone and we'll call around.'

'Art, I haven't seen her since last night. You haven't seen her this morning. I've called the school, and she wasn't in today. This is serious. I'm calling the police.'

Feeling now how dire the situation was, he agreed. 'Fair enough love.'

Sitting in the kitchen of their home, Vanessa dialled the local police station. An urgent news cast had just come onto the TV in the lounge, and Arthur tried to keep his eye on news relating to the fires. They seemed to be nearing Darfield from what he could see. Putting the phone on loudspeaker, she looked over at Joe, her son, and pointed towards the back of the house. 'Give us a minute, love,' she said, as the young boy walked out of the room with a huff.

After talking with the local police and letting them know the situation, Vanessa hung up the phone with a sigh. 'They've told me they will try to come out this way today but are flat out with calls about this weather and the fires.'

As she finished speaking, he heard a loud creaking sound emanating from the roof of their home. Arthur was still engrossed in the urgent broadcast and was becoming seriously concerned. 'This weather is getting serious, love; I need to get back out there and try to clear behind the machinery shed.' Thinking of his lost daughter, he continued. 'Try Tom. Maybe she's gone to his place?'

Tom was Arthur's younger brother and Belle's only uncle. Two years his junior, he lived in a small demountable home at the back of the Belgrove farm. Looking out at the sky, he noted it was darkening, and could see from his kitchen stool the small gum trees that lined their driveway in the distance pushed over to a 45-degree angle because of the strong winds.

'Actually, scrap that,' he said. 'I'll call him.'

Standing back in the old machinery shed at the driver's side of his ute, he called Tom on his also brand-new mobile phone. Picking up after the first ring, Tom yelled down the phone. 'Art! You guys ok? It's turning into a shitstorm out here. I'm headed towards your place, winds changing, and I think we might be in trouble.'

He could hear the wind and roar of Tom's engine through his small phone speaker, and looking outside the old shed, he could see the sky in the distance changing from a dark grey to a deep amber.

'We're all right mate, I've grabbed hose from Green's supplies and I'm hooking it directly to the new tank, I'll fill the gutters and do my best if any fire is due our way, when you get here can you jump on the tractor and try to slash the back of the shed, is your place okay? We might be lucky; it could go around us.'

'I don't like our chances Art, I just got off the phone with the Johnstone's. Fires hit their south paddock.'

That stopped him in his tracks. The Johnstone farm was directly behind theirs' and only 10km from where he was standing. Watching the wind howl inside the shed and listening to the hot tin creak above him, he remembered his lost daughter.

'Art you there?!' Tom asked.

'Yeah, I'm here,' he replied. 'Have you seen Belle today? She's not at home and hasn't been at school?'

The phone line was quiet for a short time and Tom replied, 'Haven't seen her since dinner the other night mate,' he added, 'I wouldn't stress. Maybe she's still in town?'

Not a problem he was going to solve there and then, he replied, 'Maybe. I'll see you at the house.'

As he wrestled with the long white hose his wife Vanessa had bought in town, he sweat and swore as he tried to connect it directly with the tank pump. Sweat poured off his brow as the wild wind lashed the old machinery shed. He'd never seen it this bad before, he thought to himself, as he fired up the old Honda engine again.

Pulling up at the entrance of the shed, Tom jumped out of the ute and rushed inside the old building. Over his shoulder, Vanessa and Joe came running down the back steps of the property and through the wild wind in his direction.

'Arthur!' Vanessa yelled, pointing wildly behind the machinery shed. 'Look!'

Tom looked at his brother and walked out of the shed into the open. The sky was now a blood red, and the ferocious wind battered the group as they stood outside. He watched his brother's face turn grey as he looked behind the old machinery shed. At that exact moment, tiny orange embers began to rain from the sky.

'Looks like we are out of time, brother,' Tom said in awe at the huge firestorm headed their way.

He walked out of the old shed, into now what felt like a wall of burning heat, looking out to the horizon at the back paddocks of his farm all he could see was sky high flames, he had never seen anything like it, and was stopped in his tracks at the sight. 'Ness, get Joe in the ute; we need to leave. Now!' he yelled to his wife.

Vanessa stood looking back at the house, the wall of flames now illuminating the small homestead. 'Belle! Belle?! Are you in there?' she yelled in the house's direction. 'Art, I think I saw her in the window! We've got to go back inside!'

He looked over at his wife, now with a manic look in her eyes. 'Ness, she's not in there! We were just in there! C'mon, we've got to go!'

In that split second, the large gumtree beside the machinery shed exploded in a shower of burning ember and flame. He had heard stories of bushfires and their ferocious speed, but was shocked at just how quickly it was now at his property.

'C'mon, we've got to move, there's no time!' Tom yelled at the couple.

As the wall of flames reached the back of the old machinery shed, they felt the burning heat begin to envelop the old building. With hose in hand, he valiantly tried to spray the inferno, with the small amount of water doing nothing to quell the blaze. Looking out at his childhood home, he could now see flames beginning to rise from the gutters, with the water tank beside the home beginning to melt and pour water out onto the back path, as the heat punctured its side.

Looking beyond his home, he saw what he thought was their last resort, a small dam beside the driveway they used to use for yabbies and to swim in from time to time.

'Tom, you grab Joe, Ness! The dam!' he yelled to the trio, as he broke into a run.

The group of four sprinted to the small dam as the flames engulfed the machinery shed and house. As the howling wind smashed the buildings with fire, he pushed Ness into the now lukewarm water while she screamed, 'Belle! Belle! Art, I think she's in there!'

As the four sat in the small dam up to their shoulders, he listened to his wife continue to cry out his lost daughter's name. With his childhood home now up in flames, he sat and watched the building heave and groan, engulfed in the inferno, all whilst wondering.

Where was his daughter?

Chapter Two

Nick sat in the light-filled office and looked down at his phone, which read, 10:06am. It wasn't like his superior to ever be late. There was a first time for everything, he quietly thought to himself.

Hearing the door open behind him, he placed his phone on the plate glass desk and turned around to see his boss, Mark Johnson, the Chief Inspector of the NSW homicide squad, walk in and look at him with a smile. 'Nick, thanks for coming in on such short notice. Apologies, I'm late,' he said as he sat down in his office chair and placed a handful of folders on the desk between them.

'Thanks Chief, what's this all about?'

Mark sat down and leaned back in his chair and looked Nick in the eye. While he took a sip of his takeaway cup of coffee, Nick had a feeling that something wasn't right and braced for the bad news.

'I know you've had a busy few months with this business in Milford, and now I hear you're the one that made the breakthrough in the Larson investigation?'

Nick's return to Sydney after a tumultuous few weeks in his hometown for his sister's wedding and had been quite busy. Getting straight back to work, he was one of the main investigators in the murder of Michael Larson, a fifty-six-year-old fruit and vegetable shop owner who had been shot twice in the chest, inexplicably while walking his dogs in the eastern suburbs of Sydney.

It was discovered that with crippling gambling debt, Larson's business was heading toward bankruptcy. In a last-ditch attempt to stay afloat, he had become involved with Sydney's seedy underworld, and had borrowed money from a prominent Vietnamese gang member. After failing to make repayments, he was gunned down just outside his family home.

After doggedly following leads and interviewing multiple witnesses, Nick discovered Mr. Larson's bank records and soon found a motive for murder. Through a connection he had in his earlier days on the beat in the Eastern Suburbs, he was able to find out which gang was lending money to the Sydney businessman, and after weeks of leg work finally found a prime suspect in the shooting, twenty-six-year-old

Hong Nguyen. Through multiple interviews, he finally confessed to the gangland shooting and was due in court in the following months for conviction.

'It was a team effort,' Nick said in reply to his Chief, which was true. Without the team in financial services tracking the bank records and discovering what they meant, Nick may never have got the answers he was looking for.

'Be that as it may, you have impressed people a lot higher up than me, mate. Influential people in this very building.'

Nick wondered just who the Chief Inspector was talking about. He was one of the most highly decorated in the building and on his way to becoming a commissioner.

'Thank you,' was all he could think to reply to his boss.

'I've been in this game for forty-two years now, Nick. Did you know that?'

'I remember the ceremony for your fortieth year, Chief, yes.'

'And after forty-two years, there are certain people in this building who you know you can say no to, and people in this building whom you must always say yes to.'

Nick was wondering where the Chief was heading as he continued, 'I've been asked for your services specifically,

Nick. Now I know it's only been six months since your last trip out bush and I know you've got a lot on your plate back here, but I'm sending you away again.'

Nick thought back to his last trip out bush, to his hometown, Milford. There, for his sister's wedding, he was thrown into a murder investigation and had gotten to the bottom of it. After finally getting some answers, he had spent some time investigating the cold case of his own mother's murder and had soon discovered who had ended his mother's life.

He hadn't thought he would be heading out of the city anytime soon and wondered just what the Chief needed him to do. 'Okay,' he said slowly. 'Where am I headed?'

'Darfield.'

He knew Darfield and had been through the small town in his youth. His father was a shearer and had taken Nick through the township on their way to Menindee on a hunting trip. Harsh, arid land surrounded the small town, which was right next to a large state forest. Thinking back to Darfield's history, Nick all of a sudden had a feeling why he was sitting in the Chief's office.

'Is this all because of that podcast? It's been twenty years, Chief; every man and his dog have looked into it,' Nick said.

'I agree mate,' the Chief replied, realising Nick knew exactly what case he was talking about. 'I've been requested from higher up that you take a look back at it.'

The Chief slid the case files over in Nick's direction and turned to look out the plate-glass window overlooking Sydney Harbour. 'And who knows? You might just find something.'

Nick grabbed the old case files and looked over towards his mentor. 'I'll do my best.'

'I know you will,' the Chief replied. 'That'll be all.'

Chapter Three

Belle awoke to the sound of her alarm clock and the sharp
beeping cutting through the morning air. With a grunt, she
flung her hand off the side of her bed and hit the top button,
knocking it over to the radio.

'With a top of 32 degrees, it's going to be another
beautiful day in the Mallee region. With summer around the
corner, be prepared for those temps to keep rising.'

Great, she thought to herself, with her bedroom filled with
morning sunlight, it'd be like an oven by the time she got
home in the afternoon after work. She had begged her Mum
and Dad for better air conditioning, but her Dad had said the
old swampy on the roof did the job just fine. Fat chance, she
thought, remembering the feeling of the cool, crisp air at her
friend Anna's shop.

The old homestead cracked and groaned in the scorching
morning sun, and the timber weatherboards expanded and
popped as the temperature rose. Magpies sang in the small

gumtree beside her window and from her bed, she could see the rows and rows of orange trees, ripe and ready for harvest. It was a busy time in the house, and she could hear the kettle boiling from the kitchen, and the TV on in the background.

'Belle! If you don't get up soon, you'll be late for work, love!' her Mum yelled from the kitchen.

With the weather as nice as it was, she was annoyed she'd agreed to this job, anyway. Summer was almost over, and she felt like she'd hardly had a chance to enjoy herself. 'Coming!' she called back.

The kitchen was a hive of activity. Her Dad was perched up at the table with one hand on his favourite mug of coffee and another eating a thick slice of toast, smothered in his favourite apricot jam. Her Mum was flitting about, busy making a bowl of cereal for her little brother Joe, with one eye on the TV over in the lounge room.

'They're saying the Olympic torch is going to come through Mildura,' her Dad said in her direction.

She wasn't quite sure what the fascination with the Olympics was. Everyone at school didn't shut up about it, and pretty much anything on the tv and radio had been about the Olympics for the past few months, and it was still ages away.

'Oh, right.' Was all she could think to say.

'Belle, love, you're finally up. You want some breakfast? Eat something please, you're fading away.'

Belle's weight was always a topic of conversation with her mother. She was tall and slim, from her Dad's side, and her Mum was short and a bit frumpy, she always thought to herself. She was always on a new diet and trying a new exercise routine and she hated the way her Mum spoke about her to her friends. It always made her feel uncomfortable, like she was jealous of her.

'Yeah, sure Mum, I'll have some toast.'

As she dropped down two slices of toast in front of her, Belle watched as her Mum sipped on a dark green smoothie with a grimace.

'Ugh, what is that?'

'Green smoothie love, all the ladies at the club are drinking it. You want to try it?'

Belle thought she rather be fat than drink disgusting stuff like that. 'Ahh no thanks, I'll stick with my toast.'

'Fair enough, far out! What is your brother doing in that shower? It's been 20 minutes! I swear he doesn't understand we live from water tanks!' She said, and she walked off in a huff.

Her Dad smiled over his newspaper in her direction and gave her a wink. 'Not long till your birthday love, thought any more about what you want?'

She was due to turn seventeen in just a few weeks and was excited to get her P plates on her birthday. With her friend Anna already getting her licence, it was a newfound sense of freedom that they had never had growing up in the small country town. Counting down the weeks, she had had her eye on several used cars. 'Yeah, Sam Stewart's gone off to Uni, and her Mum said they'd be selling her Ford Focus. Maybe we take a look?'

A loud ring broke through their conversation from the small mobile phone on its charger sitting on the kitchen bench. Still not used to the sound, Belle wondered how long it would be until she could get her own. A couple of the girls in her class had them and they had spent hours at lunchtime playing the snake game on the small black phones. Belle was getting quite good and was disappointed that her Dad's phone didn't have any games on his.

Standing against the kitchen bench, Belle's Dad answered. 'Morning mate, you right?'

Sitting and listening to the conversation, Belle assumed it was probably her uncle, Tom, who was two years younger than her Dad. He lived in a small demountable home at the back of their farm. He was always close by and had lived on the farm with them for as long as Belle had been alive.

'That was your uncle. I told him we were up here having brekky. He's going to come up for a bite.'

Looking at the time, she realised she was going to be late for work. 'Oh, cool Dad, I've got to be off to work now, anyway,' she said, quickly grabbing her slice of toast and making her way to the door.

Standing on the front porch hoping to see Anna's car arriving in the distance, she heard her uncle's 4-wheel drive motorbike slowing down on the back road which swept around beside the machinery shed. Coming into view and pulling up in front of the house, Tom jumped off the motorbike and smiled in her direction. Taller and slimmer than her Dad, he wore blue jeans with a torn knee and had a blue singlet on that had, 'Ettamogah Pub' printed across the front.

'Morning.'

'Hi Uncle.'

'You off to work? I thought we were gonna have brekky together?'

Looking down towards the gate, she saw the white of Anna's Dad's ute, a Mazda with a tray. 'Sorry, Anna's here. Got to go!'

As Anna pulled up, he walked over to the small ute and opened the passenger side door for her. 'Have a good day ladies,' he said through the window with a wink.

As they drove down the small gravel driveway, Anna grinned and spoke to her friend. 'I wonder why he's never met anyone. He's still pretty hot for his age.'

Belle grimaced. 'Gross Anna, he's my uncle.'

'Yeah, so what? I can still say he looks all right, can't I?'

'I don't even want to think about it,' she said, as she looked across the front paddocks of her home.

Tom had always been the cool uncle in her family and had always taken special care of her and Anna. Always around to pick them up after a party, or take them out and about and on camping trips when they were younger, she was glad that he never left the farm, as her Mum and Dad always seemed so busy.

'You reckon he'll buy us booze again for David's party?' Anna asked.

As the two girls had gone into their teenage years, Tom had started buying them alcohol whenever they needed some for a party. Anna's parents were extremely strict, and she knew what the answer would be if she asked her Mum or Dad.

'Yeah probably.'

'Good, cos my Dad would kill me if I asked him.'

After Anna dropped her off at the strawberry farm where she had picked up her summer job, Belle busied herself cleaning the small café before the lunchtime rush. The café sat at the front of the sprawling property and was always extremely busy in the spring and summer. The floor was lined with black and white chequered lino, and long glass cabinets were filled with strawberry flavoured ice creams and sweets. The front counter gleamed with neat, shining corrugated iron, and housed a state-of-the-art coffee machine, which Belle worked behind during the rush.

Finishing up mopping the floor, she began to spray and wipe the white café tables out on the front balcony overlooking the main road. As she worked slowly, enjoying the silence before the rush, she began to feel like someone was watching her. Confirming her suspicions, she jumped when she heard a rustle in the bushes down beside the outdoor table and chairs. Coming out from behind the bushes was one of her school class mates, Harry McKenzie, who was scrawny with light brown hair, and dressed in a dark jumper that looked way too big for him. He casually walked up onto the outdoor patio and smiled in Belle's direction. 'Hi Belle.'

'Ah, Hey Harry,' she replied awkwardly.

How did he get out here this early in the day? She knew he had the hots for her; he had told another one of her girlfriends, and she had made it clear back to her that she wasn't interested.

'You working today?' he asked.

Holding the bottle of spray and wipe up, she looked blankly in his direction. 'Certainly looks like it.'

'Oh, cool.'

Standing in the silence, she looked at him more closely. He wore blocky, black skate shoes with three-quarter-length jean shorts. His black hoodie had the logo SMP on it. A skate brand, she assumed. How he still wore a hoodie in this heat was beyond her. As she stood there, she could feel the morning sun already burning her. Turning back towards the shop, she noticed the owner Gino starting up the coffee machine. With a smile and a wave in his direction, she turned back to Harry. 'Well, I better get back to it.'

'Okay, ah, yeah. I'll see you at school I guess,' he replied, and with that, he turned and walked off back beside the café the way he had come.

Such a weirdo, she thought to herself. He gave her the creeps.

Chapter Four

Nick sat in the small coffee shop and looked around the room, which was painted a creamy white and was brightly lit with whitewashed tables and chairs. The shop was part of a chain he had been to many times back in Sydney, and he enjoyed using the busy venues to sit and read through case files. He hadn't been in Mildura for many years but felt like the city had changed little since his early days on the job. Sitting in the corner of the shop, he looked out at the people enjoying their morning coffees.

There were Mums who had just completed school drop off, activewear clad, with hair and makeup looking pristine. The elderly, who Nick knew would spend many hours sitting and chatting, they had nothing better to do. And finally, diagonally across from him, sat a couple around ten years younger than him.

Watching them eat quietly, he noticed that the man had spent most of his meal on the phone, scrolling mindlessly on the small screen. With his hat pulled down low and a thick brown beard, the woman sitting across from him, he could see from a distance looked shrunken, like a dog who had been yelled at too many times. Through closer inspection, he could see bruise marks across her left wrist as she sipped her coffee, and from what he could see through many thick layers of foundation, sported a black eye.

As they got up to leave, he noticed the man turn and walk back to the counter to pay. With the smallest indications, Nick caught her eye and mouthed, 'Are you ok?'

With a small, sad smile and a nod back in his direction, she replied, 'I'm fine.' It was the best he could do in the situation, he thought.

After sitting and thoroughly reading the case files he had been given by the Chief, Nick got back into his unmarked police car and pressed the start button. Scrolling through his phone he found the podcast app and typed, 'Into The Flames – the story of Belle Smith.' Coming up immediately at the top of the charts, he clicked on the first episode and indicated out towards the main highway.

He settled in for the short 70km journey and turned the volume up on his steering wheel as he navigated a tight bend just outside a sprawling grape vineyard, and settled in to listen.

'My name is Prue Thornton, and I am your host. On this season of Into The Flames, we will discuss the famous disappearance of seventeen-year-old schoolgirl Belle Smith from the small country town Darfield, in the Mallee region. A nationwide mystery, this story had captured the heart of the nation, during a summer of the worst bushfires Australia had ever seen.'

Nick slowed at a T intersection and indicated right. Turning onto the state highway, he sped up to a comfortable speed and continued listening.

'Darfield, the year 2000, the farming town was thriving due to an usually early and wet winter, and was bearing the fruits of their hard work, literally. The main farming in this region was mandarins and oranges, and because of their newest creation, the Darfield orange, farmers in the region were pulling in record profits because of its ever-growing popularity with the Asian market.'

'Seventeen-year-old Belle Smith, daughter of mandarin and orange farmers, Arthur and Vanessa Smith, was just beginning her final year of school in the small farming community, with the year twelve group in the local high school now whittled down to only fifteen students. Tall and thin, with sandy long blonde hair and hazel eyes, her face was soon on the television screens and in newspapers of every man and woman in the nation. A face forever young, etched into the nation's consciousness.'

Nick knew the face well. He remembered seeing it on his TV screen when he was younger and remembered the relentless news coverage and newspaper articles that seemed to go on for months.

'After a record season of rain for the farming community, in a cruel twist of fate, one of the worst seasons of bushfires on record had spread wildly across New South Wales, and in February, the final month of summer, the fire had set its sights firmly on Darfield and the surrounding areas.'

'As the brutal fire spread across the farms surrounding the small town, the Smith family fought to no avail against the blazing inferno, with Arthur Smith spending the morning and into the afternoon trying valiantly to fireproof their small property. Vanessa Smith spent the morning in town, with Belle's little brother, Joe, desperately buying supplies to help her husband fireproof the small home.'

Nick also remembered the coverage of the inferno across the state back then, with record temperatures in the summer, the bushland had dried unusually fast after the wet winter, and along with extremely high winds had meant that it had spread at a breakneck speed, killing forty-two people. It was the worst bushfire Australia had seen since Ash Wednesday in 1983.

'Later on, that same day with a change in wind direction, the blaze roared towards the Smith's small farm, Belgrove, with Arthur, Vanessa, Joe, and Arthur's brother, Tom, only managing to survive by running and waiting out the blaze in their small dam at the entrance to their property.'

'After two gruelling hours huddled together in the shoulder-deep, now boiling water, the Smith family emerged from the dam to find their family home now a ruined, burnt shell. With Belle due home from school that afternoon, their main priority soon became searching for the whereabouts of their lost daughter.'

'Calling around to Belle's friends and with the help of Darfield's police, it was soon discovered that Belle had not attended school that day, and fears now became that she had never left their small property, and may have been trapped inside the now destroyed home.'

'What happened to Belle Smith? Did she die during the blaze in her family home at Belgrove, the Smith's small citrus farm? Or was she taken by an opportunistic person on the hunt for a naïve schoolgirl? On this season of Into The Flames, I hope over the next five episodes to highlight the many rumours, innuendo, and discrepancies in this famous case, and with interviews with locals and family members I will delve deep and do my best to find justice for Belle Smith.'

Nick noticed deep grey clouds rolling in over the horizon. Already getting dark this early in the afternoon, he wondered just what he was getting himself into. He had read all the articles of the Belle Smith case and now had read the case files given to him by the Chief. Seventeen years old and in her final year of school, she had vanished without a trace, and it didn't seem like they had much to go on.

News reports of the time tried their best to blame Arthur Smith for the disappearance due to the fact that he had had a criminal record from his youth. Reading his record himself, Nick knew it seemed to be for only minor offences, traffic violations, and petty theft. Nothing that warranted the accusation and vitriol of most of the Australian public back at the time.

Small droplets of water formed on Nick's windscreen as he reached the outskirts of Darfield's state forest. Towering gum trees enveloped his car soon after, with the leaf coverage protecting him from the worst of the now heavy rain. Without touching any buttons, his BMW automatically sensed the rain, and the windscreen wipers began dutifully doing their job. Soon the car will drive itself, he thought to himself with a shake of his head.

Breaking through the dense tree cover, he slowed as he looked left across at the town sign. 'Welcome to Darfield', it read in neat, bright red script. He hoped this trip to the outskirts of the outback wouldn't be like his last trip to the bush.

Chapter Five

Pulling into the small general store, Nick noticed a single fuel pump standing in solitude, with thick concrete on either side patched where it looked like three more pumps used to stand. Getting out and stretching, he ran his eye over the old general store. A long single-storey weatherboard building, it had a faded red corrugated iron roof with 'Darfield General Store' painted across the top of it in now chipped and faded white paint. Around the perimeter of the old store was a tired-looking pergola, with cracked and warped spotted gum decking and a worn green painted balustrade.

As he made his way up the small steps that led onto the pergola, he looked across at the small community noticeboard nailed up beside the front door of the store. Like all buildings in country towns like this one, he noticed the same usual advertisements. 'Come and try tennis – The Darfield Tennis Club Friday night tennis comp,' and, 'Horse manure for sale, $5 a bag, or $20 for five bags.'

One notice on the board, however, caught his eye. Now faded yellow with the bottom right-hand corner slightly torn, it was the same photo used across the nation, in newspapers, and now spread across the internet of a forever seventeen-year-old Belle Smith. With her smile slightly crooked and, although the poster was in black and white, Nick knew, those shining hazel eyes. 'Have you seen this girl?' It read in large block letters. 'Last seen at Belgrove on the morning of February the 13th. If anyone has information, please contact the following numbers.'

Nick noted the names and the two separate numbers on the bottom of the flyer, Vanessa Smith and Maz Rogers.

'Help you?' said a woman, who was watching him look at the missing poster, standing at the entrance of the store.

'Sorry, yes, I think you can,' he replied.

'Look buddy, if you're one of these podcast buffs I don't know anything, never met Belle Smith, don't know her family. I'm just looking after this store for the weekend,' she said to Nick, which he felt sounded perfectly rehearsed.

Nick looked at the woman more closely. Short and slim, with denim overalls on and a small black singlet underneath, she wore a pair of old, worn-out steel-capped Blundstone boots that looked like they had seen better days. She had blonde hair cut into a neat bob and wore glasses, and she had a light smattering of freckles across her nose and cheeks. Nick thought she looked around his age, and if local, definitely would've known Belle Smith.

Nick smiled warmly at the store owner. 'I can assure you I'm not a podcast buff. Detective Sergeant Nick Vada,' he said with an outstretched hand.

Nick noticed her façade falter slightly at his words. 'Police? What's a detective doing in Darfield?'

'That I can't tell you for now,' Nick said in reply. 'And do I get a name?'

'Oh, sorry,' she said with a small shake of her head. 'Anna Denholm, please, come in.'

'Pleasure to meet you, Anna,' he said as he followed her into the general store.

He walked through the security screen door of the general store and looked inside at the old building. Black and white chequered lino covered the floor with a worn trail around the two solitary aisles that led to the register. Looking up, he saw faded advertisements for Chiko rolls and ice cream flavours he knew had gone out of existence in the 80s.

'My apologies,' Anna said in his direction. 'You have no idea how many weirdos we have had through here since that bloody podcast.'

'I'd believe it,' Nick replied as he looked inside the old fridge at the row of freshly made sandwiches. He hadn't eaten since breakfast, and they actually looked surprisingly good.

'Made fresh today,' Anna said. 'I make all the food here fresh each morning before we open. Ever since I got rid of those front petrol bowsers, the foods been keeping me afloat. Get a lot of tradies and farmers popping in for smoko and lunch.'

Nick grabbed a delicious-looking chicken salad sandwich and a bottle of water from the fridge and made his way back over to the counter. 'Don't suppose you know where the police station is from here?'

Anna ran the water bottle across the scanner. 'Another kilometre down the road, make your first left after the pub. That'll be $10.50,' she said with a smile.

'Thank you.'

'You know,' Anna said to Nick's back as he walked towards the old screen door. 'You are the first stranger through these doors this year, that hasn't asked me if I knew her.'

'Not my place to pry,' Nick said, and then continued, fairly sure of the answer, asked, 'So, did you? Know her?'

Anna casually leaned against the front counter of the shop and looked at Nick. Replying with a brief sigh, she said, 'Yeah, I did. She was my best friend.'

Jumping back in his car and heading towards the town centre, Nick looked at Darfield's streets. Not thriving, but a lot more shops were open than some of the other farming towns he knew well. He was glad to see that one rural community seemed to be sticking around.

Turning left just after what he could see was the Darfield Hotel, he made his way down the side street and parked at the entrance of the local police station. A red brick building with white bars across the front window, it sat in the shade of three enormous gum trees. With only one marked police car at the front of the building, a Holden Rodeo divvy van, Nick wondered how many officers manned this small station.

Nick walked into the entrance of the warm police station, happy to be out of the now constant rainfall. He walked through the front door and into the entrance of the small building and found no one manning the front desk. Looking through the glass which protected the reception counter, he could see into the back offices a woman talking on the phone, sitting with her feet up on the desk.

'I know Bev. I've been around there twice now, yep, yep, I know I know.' She spoke in a low, husky voice, with her notepad sitting beside her keyboard as she jotted down notes in shorthand. Putting a finger up, she mouthed to Nick, 'One minute.'

He leaned against the old reception counter and waited patiently. Finished with her call, she walked over and unlocked the reception door, and ushered him into their office. Looking at the older officer, he guessed she was in her early 60s, with dark brown hair showing slight streaks of grey through it. Short and stockily built, he read her name tag fixed to just above her front shirt pocket. 'Senior Sergeant Maz Rogers,' it read.

Maz looked at Nick with a smile and shook his hand. 'Detective Vada, I assume? Just who did you piss off to be sent out here for this?'

Nick liked her already. She didn't seem like a bullshitter, and he replied, 'Beats me, and you must be Sergeant Rogers?'

Maz looked down at her name badge and smiled. 'Great detective skills. I can see why you've been sent.'

Nick laughed and gestured at the empty offices. 'Looks busy today? How many have you got working out of here?'

Maz rolled her eyes. 'Very funny. Just the three now. We were an eight-man team for many years, but budget cuts and retirements mean that it's just me, Pat, and Samantha working here now.'

Nick looked at the three small desks in the open plan office and decided to cut to the chase. 'So, I'm guessing you know why I'm here?'

'Yep, got a call from Sydney to say you're here to investigate the Belle Smith disappearance, which means one, you've either done something to upset someone. Or two, someone higher up the food chain has been hassled.'

Nick thought back to his chat with the Chief. 'I'm guessing it's more the latter.'

Maz looked at the detective closely. In his late 30s, he was tall and well-built. His hair had a light speckle of grey through it which matched the stubble on his face, and he had blueish-green eyes. She had heard of his exploits earlier in the year through the grapevine and had looked him up on the system when she heard he was on his way. With an exemplary arrest record, he seemed to be a rising star in the force, and she wondered just why he'd been sent out here to look into a case that she knew was as cold as they got.

'Well, you may as well get started. Follow me.'

Walking through the large, open office area, they made their way down a short hallway to a doorway on their left. Putting a key in the old lock, the mortise groaned and creaked as she wiggled it back and forth. 'Bloody thing, this door doesn't get opened too often these days,' she said as she gave it a shove with her shoulder.

Walking into the storage room, she pointed at the old white shelving on the right-hand side wall, which was full of cardboard boxes. 'A good place to start.'

'Which of these boxes is the Smith case?' Nick asked.

'All of them.'

Neat, white archive boxes were stacked across the old shelving, numbered from one to fifteen. Grabbing the first box and sitting down at the small table in the centre of the room, he wiped the thick layer of dust off the top of it and lifted off the lid.

'Well, you certainly don't muck around. You want a coffee?'

Nick smiled. 'Black, please.'

Sitting now in the open office with boxes spread across two desks, he sipped his coffee thoughtfully and spoke to Maz. 'Were you here when she went missing?' he asked.

'Yep, I've been here my whole career. My son Eric was in the year below her, it was absolutely terrible back then, the fires kind of overshadowed everything for the first few weeks, but when we couldn't find a trace of her and the media got wind, it was just a madhouse.'

'So, you were involved in the search?'

'Yep, I took the call from Vanessa Smith the day she went missing. Just before the fires hit. She was beside herself. We obviously were flat out with the fires and trying to help so many people, then it all just blew up.'

Nick had read the case file thoroughly but knew that they usually only told half of the story.

Maz continued, 'Once the fires were out, the next day we went out to the farm with a search party and checked the entire property. Well, what was left of it, anyway.'

'And the house? No signs of a body?'

'Checked by the rural fire service and crime scene services. It's all there in the files. She was just gone.'

'So, what do you think happened?'

Maz sighed. 'I remember speaking to a firefighter that morning as we searched through what was left of the machinery shed and the house. He said that at the centre of that blaze it gets to one thousand degrees. One thousand, can you believe that?'

He could sense what she was saying.

'I think she never left that house, and that fire took her away.'

Chapter Six

Maz Rogers had taken Vanessa's call the day previous, and hadn't thought much more of it until the next morning when her Sergeant walked into the police station. She and her husband Dan had only just bought the local pub, a harebrained scheme of Dan's she thought at the time, and had spent most of the afternoon and night trying to save it from the fires that had ravaged their small community. The Sergeant's face was covered in ash and he looked like he hadn't slept a wink. Everyone in the station looked that way, she thought to herself as she looked around the room.

The Sergeant's expression was grim, and although she was only a few years into her policing career, she had developed a good working relationship with him. He was in his late 60s and never hesitated to tell the team that his days were numbered. She saw the opportunity to step up, and hoped when the time came, he would give her a chance.

'Got a call from Arthur Smith this morning. He said his daughter Belle is missing?' he asked in Maz's direction.

Sergeant Tom Collins also doubled as the captain of the local SES and had spent his afternoon on the eastern side of town, trying to stop the roaring inferno from reaching the main street. Their plan had worked only just, with the only buildings affected being the back of their pub and the rear of one of the local cafes.

Maz remembered the frantic tone in Ness's voice but chalked it up to Belle just losing track of time, and then with how bad the reports were of the fires, she assumed she had probably just hung back at a friend's house and hadn't got onto her parents yet.

'Sorry Sarge, I should've told you earlier, Ness Smith called early yesterday before we knew how bad it was going to get.'

The Sergeant waved her off. 'Circumstances were a bit out of our control yesterday kiddo, don't worry about it. Why don't we head out there and have a chat with them?'

'Yep, it was the first job on my list today.'

'How bad is the pub?'

She sighed. 'We've lost the back five boarding rooms, that's for sure. It got to the back wall of the restaurant, but we stopped it there. Dan's there now with Mick and Shane cleaning up.'

'I'm sorry.'

'Don't be. Thanks to your hard work, we didn't lose too much.'

'We did our best with what we had. A lot of the farms out of town lost a lot more than we did.'

The Sergeant turned as he heard the door open and watched as Rita, their receptionist, walked in. Maz knew she was close with Vanessa Smith, and she looked like she had been crying.

'You okay Rita?'

Between sobs, Rita replied, 'Th-th-they lost it all, the house is gone, and they still haven't heard from Belle.'

'Shit.' The Sergeant replied. 'They lost the house as well? I thought it might have gone around them.'

Maz consoled Rita as she sat beside her and handed her tissues as she cried. 'C'mon, let's get out there and figure this out.'

They made their way out together in the Sergeant's police vehicle and surveyed the damage across the town as they went. The local pool building was gone, now just a hollowed shell, the vintage red bricks now a scorched black. The trees surrounding were also left completely bare, with only the thick blackened trunks left to protect the old building.

'Johnstone's Winery out behind south road is gone, café and all.'

The winery was Maz and Dan's only opposition in town, but they still got along well with the owners, Dianne, and John. When they had run short of beer months earlier, they had loaned them a pallet to get them through a busy period.

'Poor Dianne, I can only imagine what she's going through. It's hard enough with what we've lost behind the pub. I don't know where any workers or tourists are going to stay now.'

'Problem for another day,' the Sergeant replied.

The phone in the cradle behind the handbrake in the police vehicle started to ring, interrupting their conversation. It'd only been installed the month previous, and she was fairly sure it was the first time it had ever rung in the car. She felt awkward holding the blocky receiver in her hand and preferred the UHF radio that they used every day. 'Constable Rogers, speaking?'

'Maz it's Charlie. I'm just getting to the Smiths now. A couple of us thought we would come out and give you a hand to have a look around.'

Before he could answer Maz's next question, he continued, 'John Sexton called around and said Arthur Smith's daughter is missing. Thought you could use our help.'

Charlie Timewell owned the local hardware shop in town, and Maz knew from their drive out that it had been saved thanks to the Chief and the SES's hard work. He was an extremely generous businessman around town, and she was surprised he would offer his services to the Smith family, considering their reputation. He continued, 'I couldn't imagine what it would be like to lose my Jessie, unthinkable. We'll see you out here.'

'Who was that?' the Sergeant asked.

'Charlie Timewell, he's got a group heading out to the Smiths to give us a hand having a look around.'

The Sergeant's gaze never left the road ahead. 'Hmm,' he replied.

Pulling down the dirt road which led towards the Smith's house, they looked out across the paddocks at the McKenzie's property. The house was still intact, along with the rear main machinery shed, although both were blackened and looked worse for wear.

'McKenzie's look like they were lucky,' she said.

'A lot luckier than most.'

Heading down the dirt driveway toward the Smith's homestead, Maz and Tom were shocked at the sheer ferocity of the fire. The front paddock on which the driveway snaked through was charred black, and the small eucalypts which lined each side were stripped bare.

Pulling into the widest section of the driveway between the main shed and homestead, there was a menagerie of different vehicles spread out. A couple of farmers' utes, a yellow SES Toyota Landcruiser, and two wagons. The group had congregated at the back tray of the SES vehicle, and she could see Vanessa Smith and Arthur Smith among them.

Before they got out of the car, Tom spoke, 'We need to tread carefully here. Everyone is on edge and Arthur Smith has a bit of a mean streak. Let them do the talking.'

She nodded and got out of the car. The heat from the day before was still thick in the air, and everything smelt like it had been burnt through twice. She winced at the smell and wiped her nose, and let the Sergeant do the talking as they walked over.

'Morning all, Vanessa, Arthur, can we have a minute?'

Vanessa Smith turned around and looked like she hadn't slept a wink from the day before. Her forehead was covered in ash and her eyes were blood red. She had streaks through the ash on her face and Maz wondered just how many more tears she had left to cry. She nodded in their direction and grabbed Arthur's hand and lead him towards them. Arthur's face was ashen and expressionless. He was a man of action she had heard and knew that he wanted to be out there looking and not talking.

'Morning. Now I've heard you spoke with Constable Rogers yesterday and we apologise we couldn't get out any sooner. Half the town needed us. Can you tell us what happened?'

Vanessa took a deep breath and wiped the tears from her eyes with the back of her old jumper. Maz looked at the poor woman and realised she probably had no clothes. With her house gone, she had nothing. She couldn't even imagine what that would be like.

'I went into town in the morning to get Art some supplies. I went in early because I knew it would be a madhouse. I took Joe and was in town at eight. Art stayed back and was prepping for the fires. Mind you, we thought nothing was going to happen. We've had plenty of fire warnings in the past. I guess we were wrong.'

Maz noted that as Vanessa spoke, Arthur was looking more and more agitated. Beginning to shift impatiently from side to side, he broke in over his wife. 'Why are we wasting our time now? You lot should've been here yesterday. Have you set up any roadblocks out of town? She's probably in the boot of someone's car right now as we speak!'

She could feel his anger as he puffed his chest up in the Sergeant's direction. She could see that Tom was getting agitated, and he tried to remain calm. 'Arthur, look around us mate, there's only two of us here. Half the town's gone. You and I both know we were occupied yesterday. As for the roadblock, let's just continue with the details for now. We are here to help. If I think a roadblock is required, I'll call one up.'

That seemed to appease the farmer, and he stepped back beside his wife, as she continued, 'Like I was saying, Art was slashing and filling gutters, and I was in town. Belle had been out and about the day earlier and had got home late, but she had school the next morning. She got herself ready these days and usually Anna came out and grabbed her. I assumed she had gone to school when I got back, but once I spoke with Art and he said he hadn't seen her, I was beside myself. I thought she might be in the house.'

She looked out across Ness's left shoulder at the smouldering wreckage of their home. The trusses were still up, and they sat precariously on the pitch-black charred frame. The gardens that she knew had surrounded the house were completely flattened into nothing. She still couldn't believe the power of the fire and how it could so quickly take away a whole family's lifetime of memories.

'When's the last time you both saw her?'

'We were on the couch watching a movie and she came in through the sliding door in the kitchen. She didn't say much, but I wished her good night and she gave me a wave.' She broke into silent tears again, and Arthur wrapped his arm around her shoulders. 'That was the last time I saw her. I should've told her I loved her.'

'You didn't know Vanessa. Let's just hope this is a misunderstanding,' The sergeant replied.

'What about your brother, Arthur?' Maz asked.

'Tom? He's back at his place, checking out the damage. He's gonna head up shortly and give us a hand.'

Odd that he wasn't with the main group, but she tried to keep her mind open. She had never been involved in anything this serious before and wanted to impress the Sergeant.

'When did he last see her?'

'We all had dinner Tuesday night, probably then, I guess,' Arthur replied.

'We'll need to ask him a few questions as well.'

'Fine.'

Maz looked at the couple huddled together and couldn't imagine what they were currently going through, their house gone, their farm destroyed and their eldest daughter missing. It couldn't get much worse.

'Ness, if you or your husband need any clothing, supplies, anything at all, please come by the pub today and we will sort something out all right?'

Ness wiped fresh tears from her eyes. 'Thank you Maz. I appreciate it. I think we will be staying with Rita for now.'

She could see their son Joe in the distance, playing in the gravel with some toy cars, and she broke off from the sergeant and the couple and made her way over. He was kneeling in the dirt by himself and had a few small matchbox cars spread around in a circle like a racetrack.

'Hi Joe, I'm Constable Rogers. You doing okay?'

The small boy looked up and she could see that he, too, had been crying. 'Hi. Have you found my sister?'

'No mate, I'm sorry not yet. Did you see her in the morning before you went into town with Mum?'

The little boy looked back down at his cars again and pushed one in an arching circle in the gravel. She didn't want to push, but knew with kids' memories they can be lost a lot quicker than adults.

'I heard her that night in her room. I didn't see her in the morning,' he said finally.

'Ok mate, thank you for that. We'll find her.'

She stood up and reached the sergeant, who was now standing by himself, closer to the wreckage of the house.

Standing beside him was a tall man who looked to be in his late forties with bright yellow firefighting pants on.

'Constable, this is the rural fire service inspector, Paul Heenan. He's been sent out to have a quick look through the house.'

'Morning.'

He smiled in Maz's direction. He was tanned and looked extremely fit for his age. He had tight lines around his eyes and his short hair was greying at the temples. He shook her hand and had a firm grip, with softer hands than she was expecting. 'Morning, I'm going to have a poke around and let you know what I find.'

'Thanks, Paul,' The sergeant replied.

Maz and the sergeant walked away from the group and watched as Paul went to work through the wreckage. He was cautious and precise in his movements, doing his best to not deter any of the burnt materials. He had a small pole that he used to poke and prod at things, and he slowly made his way through room by room.

'What do you think?' she asked her boss.

He pulled a cigarette out of his pocket and lit it. 'Too early to tell. I think the fact that she hasn't contacted them is a big worry. I'm going to speak to Mildura and see if we can get a couple of detectives up. This could become something big.'

Chapter Seven

Maz left Nick in the old archive room to himself for the rest of the afternoon, and soon he looked down at his watch and saw how late it was getting. She had left him a key of his own and he left the small police station as the sun had begun to set behind the murky grey sky. The rain had subsided, and the puddles on the road and gutters shone in the fading light. Turning around, he made his way back towards the Darfield hotel, hoping for an early dinner and to ask if they had accommodation. Pulling into the gravel carpark beside the hotel in front of a giant Victoria Bitter sign, he got out and looked at the old heritage building.

Sprawling across the entire residential block, the vintage red brick building looked to be in pristine condition. With fresh white paint across the parapet, *Darfield Hotel* was neatly written in large black block letters along the roofline.

Growing from garden beds across the base of the front walls in the footpath, the pub was covered in bright, lush green hedging, which was neatly trimmed around the windows. The two windows beside the front door had *Darfield Hotel* expertly painted in neat sign-writing on them, and looking directly above the front door set on the corner of the building, he read the same year, 1857, that he seemed to see on a lot of the old country pubs he came across, it was like the country had decided in the mid-1800s that every town needed a pub.

Walking into the old hotel, he came across a busy scene. The bar had people sitting up on old silver stools, with a barman who looked to be in his 60s, sporting a neat, brown beard and forearms full of faded tattoos, manning the frosty taps. Directly behind him was a small bistro, with tables full of hungry locals, enjoying the local pub fare.

Seeing Nick at the end of the bar, the elderly barman made his way over. 'Nick, I assume?'

'News travels fast around here,' he replied with a smile.

'Dan Rogers,' the elderly barman said with an outstretched hand. 'Maz called just before and said you might be in.'

'Nick Vada,' he replied, shaking his hand. 'She sounds like a busy woman, runs the police station, and marketing for the local pub.'

Dan chuckled. 'She'd want to recommend us. She half owns the place.'

Nick groaned internally. Rogers, of course. 'Dan Rogers. Maz is your wife, I assume?'

'She said you were a good detective,' he said, his tone dripping with sarcasm.

'Do you guys have any accommodation here? Looking for a room.'

'We used to. Before the fires. Before the whole back half of the pub burnt down. I spent fourteen hours on a hose that day trying to save it. This is all that's left,' he said with his arms outstretched.

'Bugger, is there anywhere else in town with rooms?'

'Sadly no, the motor inn closed down a couple of years back. Most people only pass through here. But look, I know why you're in town. We've got two caravans out back that fruit pickers use during harvest. Happy for you to stay in one of them if you'd like?'

Nick had stayed in his fair share of terrible old country hotels and motels and thought that sleeping in an old caravan would be no different. Wasn't like he had any other choice though.

'Sounds good to me.'

'Perfect, you hungry?'

'Starved.'

Sitting on one of the chrome bar stools at the bar, Nick tucked into an expertly cooked porterhouse steak and sipped on a cold beer whilst looking at the décor around the old hotel. Directly above the bar fridges, which ran across the back wall of the bar, were multiple giant fish heads. Mounted proudly on display below was a photo of a much younger Dan, holding one of the giant fish proudly in his arms. Nick had fished a lot with his father when he was younger and had fond memories of his time on the ancient waterways, sitting and listening for the jingle of the small bells attached to the end of his rod.

As he finished his beer, he put $100 cash down on the bar and spoke in Dan's direction. 'The start of my tab.'

'No worries, mate.' He grabbed a small key from beside the cash register and placed it on the bar. 'Sorry I can't show you around, it's just me in the bar tonight, head towards the toilets at the back and it's the first door on your left, the white Millard under the paperbark tree.'

'Thankyou.'

Walking back through the pub and on into the backyard, he found the old, white Millard caravan nestled under a towering paperbark tree. Pushing the small key into the lock, he was pleasantly surprised to find a neat and organised interior, with wood grain veneered panelling and a clean kitchenette.

Sitting down on the firm double bed, he rubbed his temples and noticed a small leak in the ceiling over the top bunk bed at the other end of the caravan. Looking at his watch, he read the time: 9:00. With his mind racing still with questions from the stack of archive boxes and conversation with Maz Rogers, he pulled out his iPhone, and found episode two of Into The Flames. He lay down on the firm mattress and closed his eyes and began to listen.

'This is episode two of Into The Flames, and I am your host, Prue Thornton. In this episode, I will discuss the main characters in the disappearance of Belle Smith, and interview her former school friend Harry McKenzie, who has never stopped questioning, just what happened to his friend.'

Nick rolled over and pulled out his notepad from the side pocket of his overnight bag and scrawled. 'Harry McKenzie?'

'Let's start with the Smith family. Vanessa, aged thirty-eight at the time, was originally from Mildura and had grown up on her parents' apple farm. Leaving Mildura at eighteen, she attended university at the University of Melbourne, and after three years, attained a diploma of nursing in 1983.'

'Moving back to Mildura, she began her working career at the small local hospital and met her soon-to-be husband, Arthur Smith, during her first year on the job after coming in late on a Saturday night with a particularly nasty cut above his left eye, that needed stitches. After treatment Arthur asked the young nurse out on a date, and the rest, they say, is history.'

'After a brief romance, the pair were married quickly and decided to leave Mildura and move to the citrus farming town, Darfield, which was Arthur's hometown. Soon after, the Smiths moved into Belgrove, a small 50-acre citrus farm on the outskirts of town, which after Arthur's parents had passed away, was given to him and his younger brother, Tom.'

'Life was good for Vanessa in the beginning. Living in Darfield, she was a pillar in the community. Working part time at the local doctor's surgery, which is now closed, she was a member of many committees and was well liked from all accounts.'

'Giving birth to a daughter, Belle, and then a son, Joe, life was good on the farm. With the orange business providing great profits for the young family before the fires.'

He pictured the young family on the small citrus farm, happy and thriving. The farm running well, keeping them all busy and both kids engrossed in schooling. Life couldn't get much better. It all made Belle's disappearance even that more confusing.

'Now, moving on to Arthur. His story is a little murkier and was subject to many popular debates in the nation back during the disappearance.'

Nick remembered back to a now famous, heated 60 minutes' interview, with Arthur and Vanessa being asked some hard questions. Arthur had stood up and smashed the boom microphone mid interview in a fit of rage. The vision was replayed across every news screen in the nation for the next month. A father grieving, and supposedly searching for answers, what had made him snap? And was he capable of that violence on his own family? It was a question still unanswered to this day.

'Arthur, aged forty-four at the time of the disappearance, had had a far more interesting youth than Vanessa. Leaving Darfield aged sixteen, he moved to Melbourne, and after spending his first year working on the docks as a labourer, was soon involved in the ship painters and dockers union.'

'In and out of trouble with the police, for at the time minor offences, I can now confirm he was arrested for a brief period in 1978, under suspicion of the kidnapping and bashing of prominent liberal member Doug Zimmer's daughter, Tully Zimmer.'

That was not a part of the files Nick had read earlier that day. Bar fights and petty thefts were one thing. But the kidnapping and assault of Tully Zimmer was a notorious case in Melbourne's painters and dockers' sordid history, with prime minister Malcolm Roberts personally getting involved at the time. With the entire of the Victorian police force put on notice, two perpetrators were eventually caught and sentenced to 25 years for the horrible crime. To be associated with that crime put Arthur on a whole different level of criminal.

'Arrested at the time, along with the two eventually convicted, Tom Steinberg and Andrew Abley. Arthur was released after an alibi was given that was supposedly rock solid. This alibi, along with many case files for the famous kidnapping, is now lost to time.'

That explained why it wasn't in any of the records he had seen. Being taken down to the station for questioning in those days was a lot more common than it was now, although not having this information in the file was an oversight on Victoria police's behalf. That information could've potentially aided investigators during the disappearance.

'This arrest was the last straw for Arthur's parents, with Arthur's father, Jack, personally driving to Melbourne and moving the wayward teenager back to a small commission unit in Mildura, closer to Darfield.'

'Getting a job in town as a diesel mechanic, Arthur seemed to straighten up his act, or so we thought. Under the Freedom of Information Act, I have managed to obtain the many run-ins Arthur had had with the Mildura police during the early 80s and up to his meeting of his wife Vanessa. I believe he was involved in a car re-bodying business, with several local Italian families, still well known in Mildura to this very day.'

'After meeting and wedding his young bride Vanessa, Arthur seemed to pick up and leave Mildura, and his life of crime behind him, with no mention of him in the Mildura or Darfield police archives until that fateful day, in the year 2000. Now was this a man who decided to play it straight, and give it all up? Or is this a man who has more secrets than any of us may realise?'

Nick knew podcasts like this knew how to grab an audience, and could make bold, outlandish claims with hardly any evidence to back them up, but thought while listening to this host Prue, two things. One, he needed to get in contact with her. And two, he needed to speak with Arthur Smith.

'As promised earlier in this episode, I have Harry McKenzie here with me to delve a little deeper into Belle, and Darfield during the time of her disappearance, Harry can you start with first, how you are connected with this case, and two what you now do for a living?'

'Hi Prue, thanks for having me on. My name's Harry McKenzie, and I was in the same year as Belle Smith in 2000 at Darfield High School. My parents' farm was close to Belgrove but was luckily spared during the fires, due to a sudden wind change. I helped search the Smith's farm with my Mum and Dad and a lot of other locals at the time once the fires had died down. As a community, we were devastated by Belle's disappearance. It's pretty much been a constant in my life since the day it happened. I've never stopped wondering, just what happened to her?'

Harry continued. 'And onto your second question, probably having a lot to do with the fact that we never got answers on this case, I am now a private investigator. I still live in Darfield but do mostly insurance works for larger corporates in the Mallee region, and sometimes venture as far as Adelaide.'

Interesting, Nick thought. He may have some local insight and may not be as biased as the police.

'So, what is your theory on what happened to Belle Smith?' Prue asked.

'I have gone back and forth on many of the different popular theories. Was she lost to the fire? Did she run away? Was she murdered by her father? Was she kidnapped by some unknown stranger? All of them. I'm still running down a couple of my own theories, but I personally think she was murdered,' Harry said.

'By Arthur Smith?'

'Yes. You just can't remove his earlier criminal record and the kidnapping of Tully Zimmer from this case. He had a history of violence against women, and although we may never know the motive, I believe he has all of the answers we are looking for.'

He thought it was a bit of a stretch, with no motive, the two podcasters were grasping for evidence that didn't just quite seem to be there yet. It had left some unanswered questions in Nick's mind about Arthur Smith, and he knew he had to keep all of his options open this early in his investigation. Putting his phone on charge, he listened to the steady patter of rain on the caravan roof, and soon fell into a deep sleep.

Chapter Eight

Rain lightly fell on the roof of the old caravan as the tired framework creaked and groaned in the wind. Nick had been having nightmares for the past few months once again of his mother's death, and now could see the killer's face, ending her life swiftly. It was a picture he had now watched in his mind a hundred times over, like a broken record.

Bolting upright, he rubbed his eyes and stared at the wood panelled veneer ceiling. With his mind now clear, he was glad to of only drank one beer the night before. He had had problems with alcohol in the past, which had all come to a head after his father's funeral a few months earlier. Since then, he had only drank sparingly and was trying his best to clean up his diet, hoping to last a little longer into retirement than his own father had. As he dressed, he looked down at the notches on his belt buckle and was happy to see it had come in two spaces. He hadn't been this light since his 20s, his mind and body thankful for the welcome change in lifestyle.

Opening the small door to the van and revealing sunshine peeking through the clouds, he made his way down the moss-covered footpath and looked out behind the caravans. He could still see the concrete slabs which housed the old rooms of the pub that had been lost during the bushfires.

Carrying a full keg up on his shoulder with ease towards the back door, Dan Rogers smiled in Nick's direction. 'Morning mate, how'd ya sleep?'

'Like a rock, actually.'

'Bit of rain on an old metal roof. Will put anyone to sleep.'

'Is there any place to have breakfast around here?'

Dan ran his fingers through his long beard. 'Yeah, sure, The Western should be opening up about now. Coffee shop, about a two-minute walk that way,' he said, pointing over his shoulder.

'Thanks.'

Nick walked out the front door of the old pub and made his way along the main street of Darfield. The footpaths were still wet and glistening after the heavy rainfall the night before. Unlocking his phone, he typed in 'Harry McKenzie Darfield' into his search bar and clicked on the top search.

Looking through the neat and professional website, he was impressed. McKenzie seemed to have quite a lot of high-profile businesses as clients, which was surprising considering he lived so remotely, but these were the times we live in these days, he remembered.

After a short walk past a small post office building, hairdressers and what looked like used to be a Chinese restaurant, Nick stood out front of The Western Café. He could smell the freshly ground coffee from the front door, and as he made his way through, he almost ran head-first into Anna Denholm.

Holding a takeaway coffee cup in her hand, she looked at Nick with a smile. 'We've got to stop meeting like this.'

'Taste testing your competitors?'

She shook her head. 'No way. These guys make the best coffee I've ever had. I don't even bother trying. Most of the people coming to my little shop aren't too picky.'

'Fair enough. I'll be able to give you a review shortly.'

'Look forward to it, see you around!' she said with a smile as she walked over to her car.

He turned back. 'Hey, would you mind if we catch up for a chat in the next few days? I'd like to know a bit more about Belle and get your thoughts on the disappearance.'

He noticed an ever so slight change in her demeanour at the question. 'Ah, yeah, okay. You know where I'll be,' she said, as she got in her car and gave him a wave.

The small coffee shop was a hive of morning activity. A young girl manned the register at the white counter, taking orders while a man and woman expertly crafted coffees one after another. The ceiling had ancient, exposed hardwood trusses running from wall to wall, with evergreen jasmine creeping through the bottom chords. Whoever had styled the café had taken a leaf out of the new wave of styling in the inner-city cafes. He felt like he had already been here before.

After finishing his breakfast, he sipped on his second latte ordered in a takeaway cup. Anna was right. The coffee was delicious, perfectly roasted, and at just the right temperature. Sitting in the bustling coffee shop, he watched a similar crowd of people around him as the day before in Mildura and wondered, just who had the pull or authority up high in the police force to have an investigator like him dragged out here? He was overqualified for this, and from what he could see with the Darfield team's investigation, it didn't seem like there were any new leads.

As he finished the last of his coffee, he noticed Maz Rogers walk through the door in uniform. 'Just the usual thanks, Alex,' she said to the young barista behind the state-of-the-art machine.

'You're out and about early,' she said in his direction.

'I'm an early riser, don't like to waste the day.'

'Right. Hope the vans out the back weren't too bad. I got Dan to give it a clean out when we heard you were headed our way. I assumed you'd like to stay close to town, no point driving back to Mildura every night.'

'Thank you, much appreciated.'

'No worries, I'm headed back to the station now if you'd like to meet the team?'

'Sounds good.'

As he drove over toward the police station, he wondered just how much policing would be required in a town like Darfield. The odd neighbourly dispute, dealing with drunks and perhaps some speeding farmers. The days would be a drag out here.

Walking into the police station, Nick was hit with the smell of wafting cigarette smoke. Maz sat at her same small desk with her takeaway coffee cup now sitting with the lid off, as she flicked her cigarette ash into it. 'Detective Nick Vada, meet Constable Pat Farlow and Constable Sam Carmichael,' she said, pointing at the two other officers standing in the station.

Leaning against the small kitchen bench, Pat spoke first. 'G'day detective,' he said, with his hand outstretched.

When Nick heard the name Pat Farlow, he was expecting someone more like Maz's age and not in his early 20s. Pat was around Nick's height, with sandy blond hair and a fair complexion. He looked like he had just got out of the academy.

Shaking hands with the young constable, Nick replied, 'Hi mate, first posting?'

Maz sensed the sarcasm. 'Pat's come to us directly from Goulburn and is very keen to learn.'

'I can see that, and you must be Sam?'

Standing beside Pat, Sam looked at the detective. 'Nice to meet you, detective,' she said with a shy smile.

Sam was further along in her policing career, Nick thought. In her later 20s, she was average in every way. Brown hair, with black-rimmed glasses, she had a serious look about her.

'Anything you need to help, just let us know.'

Maz put the last of her cigarette out in the coffee cup. 'Thankyou, you two, I'm going to show Nick the sights today. Maybe start out at the Ellison's? John called and think's Scott Broderick has moved his fence onto their property again.'

'On it sarge,' Pat replied.

As the two constables walked back out to start their shifts, Nick spoke first. 'I thought you couldn't smoke in police stations?'

Maz looked at him from over her reading glasses. 'I won't tell if you won't, detective.'

Nick hated smoking after losing his father to them. Choosing to let it go and move on, he asked, 'So, have you listened to the podcast?'

Maz sighed. 'I have.'

'And what do you think?'

'Look, it's very well done. But most of it was stuff we already knew. And a lot of wild theories and speculation.'

'What about all of this stuff with Arthur and the Zimmer kidnapping?' he asked. He was sure he hadn't seen anything about it in the case files.

'It's all speculation. I spoke with the Port Melbourne police way back when about it. They told me they never seriously looked into him for it.'

Why did he feel like she was holding something back from him? 'Fair enough,' he replied.

'The guys are going to have their hands full at the Ellisons. How about I show you around?' she asked.

'Yeah, no worries, I could use a bit of local knowledge.'

'I'll do my best. Where to first?' she asked.

'I'd like to start with Harry McKenzie, then we can head out and meet the Smiths.'

The sun had now risen to the centre of the sky, and the low cloud cover made it feel more like the middle of winter than the springtime. Heading back towards the outskirts of town under Maz's directions, light raindrops fell against the windscreen once again.

Cutting through the silence, Maz asked, 'So why do you think you're really out here?'

'I'm not totally sure, to be honest,' he replied. 'I'd say a couple of things, I've had a rough year, and someone high up either has a connection to this case or has listened to this podcast that everyone is talking about, and I'm from Milford, so I'm probably the highest ranking officer from the bush that we have in Sydney,' he said.

'You're from Milford?'

'Yep, born and bred. Moved away when I finished school. Don't go back enough, unfortunately.'

'Beautiful spot. My Dad used to take us camping up the river there.'

'There's no place better.'

'So, this podcast. How much of it have you listened to?'

'The first few episodes. Started on the way up here.'

'The host tried to get me on you know, Prue is her name, lovely young girl. She has called and emailed a few times. I've told her I'm not interested.'

Nick understood Maz's thinking. A case this famous would've lived rent free in the older officer's head for her whole life. What was the point of digging up old wounds?

'I've been on this case for 22 years,' she continued. 'I don't need someone coming in and dragging all of this back up, just to profit from a broken family's pain.'

'I get it. I guess our only hope is maybe someone comes out of the woodwork, and we get a tip off.'

'I don't think you get it, detective. After all this time? I doubt there'll be any tips. She's gone.'

Chapter Nine

The farm house on the outskirts of town sat on a small rise, once a part of a sprawling vineyard it had fallen on hard times, with the original owners selling parcel after parcel after each poor harvest, and the property soon was down to just four small paddocks, which were stark and bare. Whispers around town were that John McKenzie was a lazy farmer, and spent more time down at the local pub than tending to his dwindling vineyard.

The rainfall from the night before had managed to fill every pothole on the short gravel driveway up to the home, and Nick and Maz slowly navigated the road in silence. Pulling up to the front of the home, they got out of Nick's police car and made their way across the pristine front yard. Someone had taken care here, he thought, with freshly mowed grass around the property forming a neat perimeter. Rose bushes were spaced in even increments lining the front porch, trimmed, and expertly staked into the garden bed.

Standing on the front porch, he noticed that the front door to the old house was propped open awkwardly. Raising an eyebrow in Maz's direction, she shrugged in return.

He yelled down the long hallway. 'Mr. McKenzie? Police.'

Sharply knocking on the front door jamb, Maz shouted as well. 'Harry, Maz Rogers here! You in?'

As they waited on the front porch, Nick heard something from the back of the old home. Was that crying? 'Hear that?' he asked.

Maz nodded in reply. 'Sounds like something crying?'

Nick kept his ear out for the cry and yelled again, 'Mr. McKenzie? Harry? You there mate?'

Taking the lead, Maz stepped past Nick and headed down the long hallway. 'He wouldn't mind,' she said to Nick as she continued through.

Walking down the entrance and into the main hallway of the house, Nick noticed that there was a fine layer of dust blown across the entrance and opening to the lounge room, like the door had been left open for quite a while. He also wasn't surprised to see the interior just as neat as the garden.

The lounge room was spacious and modernised, and the old floorboards were polished to a high shine, albeit now a little dusty. Neat rugs were scattered about under expensive and modern brown leather furniture, and the huge flat-screen TV was still on, with the credits to a movie rolling across the screen. In the kitchen, the bench tops shined in the muted sunlight. The back wall was full of polished stainless-steel appliances and he noticed a sandwich sitting on a plate on top of the bench top, covered with flies with the edges of the bread starting to go blue with mould. He guessed by the decor that Harry McKenzie was a bachelor, noting that the house seemed to lack the touch of a woman, and saw no photos of a partner or kids, or any family for that matter.

Hearing the crying louder now, he realised it was coming from a dog at the back of the house. Looking over at Maz, he nodded towards the rear door.

'Something doesn't feel right,' she said.

He could feel a stillness in the air that didn't quite gel with him either, for the house to be this quiet, with the front door open and things left on, it was the sandwich on the bench that made him feel uneasy, like someone had left in a hurry. 'I agree,' he said.

Making their way out onto the back porch, he noticed that although there had been heavy rainfall the night before, the back sprinkler was left on and had flooded the grass in the backyard. Making his way over and turning off the tap, he heard the louder cry now of a dog. Pointing towards a large shed around one hundred metres from the back of the farmhouse, he took the lead, with Maz in tow.

As they made their way towards the shed, they heard the cries stop, and soon an old red kelpie slowly walked around from the side of the shed. Walking up to Maz, with its tail wagging profusely, she bent over and scratched it under the chin.

'Hey girl, are you okay? Where's your Dad?' she said to the old farm dog. Turning and walking back in the direction she came, the two followed her, dodging puddles out towards the desolate farm paddocks.

Getting toward the corner of the shed, He stopped in his tracks, seeing a blood-stained handprint on the edge of the building. Holding his finger up to his lips, he pointed at the handprint as he reached for his firearm, with Maz doing the same.

Slowly edging around the side of the shed, with their guns pointed towards the ground, they moved slowly forward, with a small trail of blood on the ground marking their route. In the distance, Nick noted that the old kelpie had stopped and sat next to a shape lying in the long brown grass.

'Harry?' Maz spoke in the shape's direction on the ground, not seeing any movement or seeing any immediate danger, they re-holstered their weapons and walked through the long grass to investigate.

With his eyes permanently fixed to the sky in a blank, expressionless stare, Harry McKenzie lay dead in his paddock, with a gaping, bloodstained gunshot wound to his chest.

Chapter Ten

Belle sat behind the counter of the old general store, and with one foot up beside the cash register, and she painted her big toenail with neat precision as she spoke, 'I don't know. He just gives me the creeps,' she replied to Anna.

'Hey, count yourself lucky. I wish I had an admirer,' Anna said.

'This is different An, he's always around, first at school and now he's at my work. It's getting a bit weird, don't you think?'

Anna looked at her best friend in admiration, and a little bit of jealousy. Tall and slim like the women in her favourite fashion magazines, she had begun to develop into a woman a lot earlier than her. And she wondered if she would start attracting the eyes of the boys in town like her.

'I guess.'

'I think I'm just going to tackle it head on. I'm gonna talk to him and tell him I'm not interested. That will do it.'

Belle had the subtlety of a sledgehammer, Anna thought, and knew she was about to break another heart. 'Go lightly. He's a bit younger than us, remember.'

'Yeah, yeah, I know. Hey, you reckon we could bum another pack of smokes?'

The girls had been grabbing packs of smokes from time to time from behind the counter of Anna's Mum and Dad's general store and were well known at school for always being generous enough to give them out.

'Yeah, good idea.'

Anna got up and slid the glass cabinet case across. She didn't really like smoking that much, but kept it up because Belle seemed to enjoy it. 'Winnie blues?' she asked.

'Yeah, whatever's weakest, those last ones gave me a head spin.'

A few hours later, the two girls sat out the front of the local fish and chip shop, eating hot chips from the oil-stained butcher's paper. Anna grabbed a big handful. She loved the salty chips and enjoyed sitting out front of the shop, people watching with her friend.

'Gee slow down a bit An, they go straight to your bum, you know,' Belle said.

She hated when Belle said things like that. It always hurt her feelings. 'Of course you'd say that. You eat all this stuff, and nothing happens. I eat it and look at me.' Looking down at the small bulge of her tummy over her shorts, she quickly dropped her handful of chips, grabbing just a single one, and tried to eat it slowly.

'I'm just playing babe.'

Anna knew her friend was just looking out for her, and there was no malice in what she said, but the words still did hurt. Belle was well known to her friends as one who didn't mince words. If she had something on her mind, she would tell you.

A dark green Ford ute pulled up suddenly out front of the fish and chip shop and the hot tip of the bonnet nearly touched the edge of the cast iron table that the girls sat at. The ute idled quietly, and Anna noticed that the sun visor was pulled down low, and she could just make out a man's eyes through the dark tinted windows, staring in their direction. After a few minutes, Belle was the first to stand up. 'Oi! We're trying to eat here!' she yelled towards the ute.

Anna had a weird feeling about the lone stranger sitting in the car. It had Queensland plates, the maroon colour on them standing out compared to the yellow and black plates of the cars around town. She hadn't seen the ute around before, and she felt a little scared. 'Belle, this guy is giving me the willies. Let's get out here.'

'Fine by me, I'm done anyway,' Belle replied to her. 'Thanks a lot! You ruined our lunch!' she yelled in the ute's direction.

As the girls stood from the table, Anna wrapped the rest of the hot chips up and made her way toward the bin. Before she made it there, the ute reversed suddenly in a rush and accelerated hard in the direction that it came.

'What was that all about?' she asked.

'Who knows, some weirdo, I guess.'

As the girls got older, Anna had begun to notice more the lingering eyes on them both, as they reached their final year of schooling. Even the older farmers would give her a wink from time to time when they stopped for fuel at her store, making her uncomfortable. Belle seemed more oblivious to it, she thought, and she worried a bit about her naïve friend as they made their way into adulthood.

'You want to stay out at mine tonight?' Belle asked.

'Yeah, okay, I'll just check if Mum needs me at the shop on the way past.'

Stopping past her parents' general store, Anna pulled up and ran up the staircase leading to the shop entrance. Repacking the shelf against the back wall with small bags of sugar, Anna's Mum, Jan, looked her daughter up and down. 'You right love?'

'All good Mum, you need me today? I was gonna go stay out at Belle's tonight if that's cool?'

'No worries hun, I think we'll close up shortly anyway, you have fun, and remember..'

'Stay safe,' Anna said, finishing her Mum's sentence with an eye-roll.

Anna and Belle had been inseparable since primary school, but Jan had heard the rumours when the Smiths moved to town. And her husband had heard even more stories in the pub over beers with fellow locals. She had known Belle's grandmother and grandfather as she grew up and knew that their farm was a profitable one, something that had continued ever since Arthur and Vanessa had taken over.

Even though the years had passed, she still felt a slight pang of unease when her daughter was out on that property. Something didn't sit quite right with Arthur Smith, and she noted she had never seen him set foot in her store. Not something she couldn't say about any other locals in the small town.

The two girls sat in Belle's bedroom after dinner and listened to the top ten countdown on the local radio station, with a cassette tape in their boombox at the ready to record their favourite new songs. Anna manned the buttons on the bottom of the stereo and waited for the precise moment to press record to ensure she missed all the ads. The bedroom was painted a light pink colour, and Belle had stuck posters from all her favourite magazines on the back wall and ceiling.

'I reckon it's gonna be hit me baby one more time again,' Anna said to Belle, while she flicked through the latest Cleo magazine.

'Yeah, either that or no scrubs.'

Anna had noticed Belle seemed quieter now back at home and wondered what was on her friend's mind. 'You all right? I don't have to stay tonight, you know?'

'Yeah, I'm fine, don't be silly,' she replied as she twirled her hair and stared up at the posters on the ceiling. 'Who do you reckon was in that ute before?'

Anna had wondered the same thing as the afternoon led into the night, and now she knew it had been on Belle's mind as well. She looked up at Belle and spoke. 'No idea, but it was weird, wasn't it? I couldn't really see his face, but like why would you just sit there staring?'

'Mmm, I'm not sure, but I feel like I've seen that ute somewhere before..'

The girl's conversation was interrupted by a soft knock at the door. Walking in with a smile, Belle's uncle, Tom, sat down at the edge of the bed with a plastic bag in hand and pulled out two four packs of lemon ruski's. 'Don't go telling your Mum or Dad or they'll bloody kill me,' he said in Belle's direction. 'I'd rather you two get it from me than some dodgy kid at a party.'

'Thanks Uncle, you know us, we're always on our best behaviour.'

'Fat chance,' he scoffed. Anna could smell alcohol slightly on his breath, sweet and pungent. 'You staying tonight, An?' he asked.

'Yup.'

'Nice. Hey, listen, I'm going camping next Friday night, out at Lake Somerstead at the caravan park, just like the old days, if you girls want to tag along?'

Anna enjoyed her camping trips with Tom and Belle. They were always allowed to have a few drinks, smoke whenever they wanted, and could be themselves around Belle's cool uncle. Looking at him sitting on the bed, she could see the smallest tuft of brown chest hair coming out of the top of his work shirt, and the slight scent of alcohol mixed with the smell of his work shirt made her think thoughts of her best friend's uncle that she never had before.

'We'd love to,' she said, answering for them both a little too quickly, with a big smile.

Chapter Eleven

Nick stood at the edge of the farm shed and watched the young constable running tape from the base of the towering gum tree, across towards the metal column that supported the edge of the machinery shed building. Rain had started to fall again on the farm, and he hoped they weren't going to lose any vital evidence before they got a chance to find it.

Maz Rogers walked back from the back of the house out to the shed. Looking at Nick, she was glad to have the seasoned investigator here, considering she had never experienced a murder in her hometown. 'Right. Well, what now?' she asked Nick expectantly.

Nick pulled his phone out of his pocket and scrolled through his contacts. 'We've secured the area. This rain is not going to help us, but I'll put in a call to headquarters and request crime scene services. I'm not sure where they are based out of around here, but might be best to leave Pat out here until we can get them onsite to look for evidence.'

Pat had wandered over to the duo and nodded in acceptance of Nick's order.

'Once we've got them here, we can head to the neighbours and ask if they have seen or heard anything in the last week. I'd say judging by the victim, the dust in the hallway, and the sandwich on the bench, it's been a few days at least.'

Standing and looking over Harry's body, he noticed it had started to bloat slightly, and the slightest trickle of foamy blood had formed under his nostrils and mouth. He was tall and thin, with brown, tanned skin, and looked to be in good shape. He wore black running shorts, an old paint-stained work shirt and was barefoot, which he thought was unusual. The soles of his feet looked scratched badly, and looking at where his body was lying, he assumed he was trying to run away when he was shot.

Looking around the surrounding area, he noted that the back paddocks of the property seemed bare, with no evidence of the existing orchards that once were the most important thing on the farm.

Maz stood slightly behind the detective and watched him closely, surveying the scene. He stood and looked closely at the body, making sure to not touch or contaminate Harry's body in any way. She had read up on his career and was impressed at his laundry list of achievements. Watching him methodically scan the vacant paddocks, lost in thought, she wondered why someone as experienced as him was sent to Darfield in the first place.

'He wasn't much of a farmer then, I assume?' he asked her as he looked out into the paddocks.

'No, not that I know of,' she replied. 'His Mum and Dad had an orchard back in the day, which looks like they've knocked down. Then they ran a few sheep, but more as a hobby. Once they passed on, it's pretty much looked like this since then. I think his private eye stuff keeps him plenty busy.'

'Has any of his work come across your radar?'

Maz pulled a crumpled pack of cigarettes out of her pocket and placed one in her mouth. With a quick flick of her lighter, she took a long inhale and then slowly exhaled. 'Apologies, I'm not used to seeing something like this. Yes, we had spoken from time to time, his bread and butter was dodgy insurance claims. Person gets injured, sues company, company hires him to keep an eye on them, he takes photos of them out enjoying their life, injury free of course, and he takes it back to the insurance company.'

'Something like that could make a lot of enemies,' Nick said.

'I guess.' She took another long inhale of the cigarette. 'Look, Darfield's a quiet place, detective. Like I said, there hasn't been a murder here in my time on the job.'

'And yet here we are.'

After getting a call back that crime scene services were an hour away, Nick and Maz left Pat to watch over the scene. Walking back towards the home, he slowed as he reached the back porch as he looked at the cream-coloured weatherboards. It reminded him of his childhood home and made him instinctually think he needed to call his sister and check in.

'Let's have a look around, see if we can see anything else before the team gets here.'

Walking back through the neat kitchen, he noticed a couple of dishes sitting in the sink. One coffee cup had lumpy greyish milk sitting in it, which looked like it had been left for a few days. It looked to him like Harry had been surprised at his visitor and unprepared for what was to come.

Maz called from another room. 'Detective, come and take a look at this.'

He walked back down the dusty hallway towards the front door and made a right through the doorway into what he assumed was a bedroom. Looking around the room, he realised it must have been Harry's home office, with a neat corner desk in the corner and an expensive-looking computer sitting on top of it. The walls were lined with whiteboards, with clients' names and photographs neatly lined up. What caught his eye, however, was the biggest board of all against the long wall, with *'Belle Smith.'* written across the top.

Spread across the board was a map of Darfield, with multiple pins placed across it. Around the outskirts of the map were various images of people he knew and some faces he didn't. All in all, it was an impressive display and showed him that Harry was a meticulous and organised person who put a lot of care into his work.

'He seems very interested in Belle Smith's disappearance, for something that happened so long ago,' he said, as he slowly read through the neat post-it notes scrawled across the board.

'Yeah, looks that way,' Maz replied.

He continued looking over Harry's impressive computer display; it looked similar to the setup he had seen in the IT department in his office and knew it would cost a pretty penny. Dual curved monitors sat on the wide glass desk, with a large keyboard lit up by green neon keys and a giant webcam sat on top of the screens, with a small red light blinking innocently in their direction.

'Just how much money was in this private eye work?' he asked.

'Beats me. From what I hear, he worked for some big companies.'

'Big enough companies to afford gear like this? Something doesn't feel right. How can someone living this far away from a major city in his line of work still have this farm and use it for nothing other than a house and still afford to live here?'

'I'm pretty sure his parents owned the property, so it would've been passed down to him, but I agree, a place even this small requires upkeep. And all of this gear looks expensive.'

Nick's phone ringing broke the silence. 'Detective Vada, speaking?'

Maz noticed Nick turn a light shade of red. Was he blushing? She noticed a slight shift in the young detective's body language as he took the call. 'Crime scene services are five minutes away,' he announced.

Standing in the now glaring sun, Nick watched as Senior Constable Bec Ranijan of crime scene services removed gear from the back of her van. Earlier the year before, she had been on the scene of a case in his hometown. He had seen her in action back then, calm and methodical, and she seemed to have extensive knowledge of all things in homicide investigation. He watched as she spoke with her colleague, a round man in his early fifties whom he hadn't met yet, and marvelled at her beauty. She had shining long black hair and coffee coloured skin with shining hazel eyes. She still had the look of a girl who put in absolutely no effort each morning, and yet effortlessly looked better than all that had. Kicking him out of his daydream, Maz walked past and introduced herself. 'Sergeant Maz Rogers and this is Detective Sergeant Nick..'

'Vada.' Bec finished with a smile in his direction.

Maz looked back in Nick's direction. 'Correct. I take it you two know each other?'

'Briefly. We worked a case over in Milford last year.'

'I heard about that,' Maz replied.

Not wanting to talk about his time in his hometown at that moment, he pressed on. 'Good to see you again, senior constable. So, I'm guessing you're not still based out of Edithvale?'

'No, transferred at Christmas to Mildura. I have some family up here.'

'Nice.'

Nick wondered silently if she had met someone since they last met, and felt words unspoken from their last meeting. She had given him her number during their first meeting, but Nick never acted on it, with his mind too busy with the problems at hand at the time. She was still way out of his league, anyway; he thought to himself.

The elderly crime scene officer behind the trio stepped forward with his hand outstretched. 'Neville Parker, heard a lot about you, detective,' he said, shaking Nick's hand with a firm grip.

He was curious to know what Bec had said about him, but knew it wasn't the time to ask. 'Nice to meet you, mate. As you can both see, our victim is just out there in the paddock. Harry McKenzie, aged thirty-one, looks like a single gunshot wound.' He pointed towards the clouds and continued, We're up against it with this rainfall but we've managed to find two quikshades in the machinery shed. Pat over there will give you a hand to put them up over the body for now. It's the best we can do. If there's anything else we can do, let us know.'

'On it.'

'We're going to speak with the neighbours, see if they have seen or heard anything.'

Leaving the two specialists to their work, he walked back over in Pat's direction with Maz. 'Where's his dog gone?' he asked.

'I think she's back in the machinery shed. I saw a kennel in there.'

Nick made his way back over towards the shed into the back of the building and found an old corrugated iron kennel filled with old blankets. The old dog was cautious of his approach, but she rose as he got to her and stretched back and pushed her front paws out straight ahead and gave a big yawn. 'Hey old girl, hope we aren't keeping you up.'

He gave her a scratch under the chin and slid her collar around to reveal her name. "Bailey."

'Pleasure to meet you, Bailey. Looks like your Dad is no longer with us. I'm going to look after you until we find you a new home.'

He had had various working dogs throughout his childhood, but his years in the city and busy career meant he couldn't have his own pets anymore. He still had a deep affection for dogs, though, and especially the working dogs of the bush. Bailey was now an orphan, he thought to himself, and he wanted to make sure she found a new home and was safe. He grabbed an old lead that sat on the workbench beside her kennel, clipped it on, and slowly lead her out towards Pat.

'Constable, once those quikshades are up, can you please take Bailey here into town? Drop her off at the pub and tell Dan I have a plus one.'

Pat blinked twice at the odd request and looked down at the old dog, whose tail was now wagging profusely. 'Of course, detective.'

Heading back over and getting into his police car, Maz jumped in beside him and quickly asked the question he knew was on her mind. 'So, I'm guessing you two have dated?'

Trying to think of a way to get out of this talk with someone he barely knew, he changed the subject quickly. 'No way, she's out of my league. Now, who are the next-door neighbours?'

Maz decided to leave it, a conversation for another time. Getting another cigarette out of her top pocket, she cracked the window down in the car and looked over in Nick's direction.

'I know, I know, do you mind?'

'Go ahead, company car.' He hated the smell of cigarette smoke and knew he would have to get his car deep cleaned when he got back to the city to get rid of the smell.

Taking another deep inhale of the cigarette, Maz braced for Nick's reaction to the next bit of information. 'Right. Neighbours. To the left, closer to town, are the Sextons. John is the local doctor, and his wife Wendy was a schoolteacher in her earlier days. Now both retired.'

'And to the right?'

Maz prepared herself. 'To the right is Belgrove. The Smith's property.'

Chapter Twelve

Well, that certainly makes things interesting, Nick thought, as he drove through the gates of the Sexton's small property. In the podcast Harry had mentioned he lived close by, why didn't he say next door?

In similar condition to the McKenzie farm, the Sexton's property had a small, neat orchard beside the right-hand side of the house, which ran back as far as the eye could see. Covered in white netting, which spanned from the driveway gate right back down on and past the house, he assumed it was in place to protect the orchard from pests. His experience in fruit farming was extremely limited, with the farming in his hometown being mostly grain.

Pulling up to the front of the house, he noticed the building was similar in style to the McKenzie property, and looked to be originally a demountable home. It stood off the ground around a metre high, with a neat balcony that wrapped around the perimeter. It was painted a light blue colour, and the windows had white trimming. The front porch was lined with evergreen pot plants, with some hanging from hooks near the gutter, and others above the metal balustrade hand railing.

Maz knocked on the door and waited. Hearing footsteps coming to the door, the two officers stepped back to allow the old screen door to swing open towards them.

'Oh Maz, how are you, love?' said Wendy Sexton, standing in the doorway with a white and blue patterned apron on. She looked to be in her seventies and was short and slim. Wearing wire-frame glasses, she had a shock of white hair on top of her head and exuded a welcoming glow.

'I'm fine thank you, Wendy, this is Detective Vada,' she said pointing to Nick and continued, 'Mind if we pop in for a quick word?'

'Of course, come in. I've just finished baking banana muffins.'

Walking into the small lounge room, it was lined with photos of the Sexton family in various stages of their lives. Babies, kids, and adults. They must have been a big family, he thought as he looked at the many images. He could smell the baking coming from the kitchen. It smelt incredible and he could feel his mouth beginning to water.

'Take a seat please,' Wendy said, ushering the two officers onto the light brown couch. 'I'll just grab those banana muffins out of the oven. Would either of you like a cuppa?'

'Yes, please,' Maz replied. He nodded as well; he had learned to never say no to food during a home interview. It helped people open up when you ate their food.

As the old woman walked out of the room towards the kitchen, he looked over to Maz and asked, 'Big family?'

'Four kids, all with kids. Three of them are in Melbourne these days, but Chris, the eldest, has a property further out of town.'

Nick remembered during his childhood in the bush all of his friends and their families. They were big back in those days, with small clans walking around the town, following Mum through the shops. With job opportunities dwindling in the bush, many of those kids grew up, and moved to the bigger cities in search of bigger and better things, himself included. Leaving the elderly and just the few loyal kids behind.

Wendy sat the big tray of banana muffins and three cups of tea down on the coffee table in front of them. He was the first to grab one and take a bite. Warm and fresh, the muffin was perfectly baked with a brown crispness on the outside and a moist and sweet centre full of banana and small pieces of chocolate.

She wore a wide smile in the officer's direction and looked happy to see them enjoying her baking. The lounge room was warm and inviting, and the scent of baking and the smell of tea took him back to his own grandmother's home in his childhood.

'Now, how can I help you two?' she asked.

'Mrs. Sexton, have you seen or heard anything unusual from the McKenzie property over the last few days?' he asked.

'From Harrys? No, not that I can remember. He's a quiet kid, to be honest. I see his car heading in and out of his driveway, but not much else. Why do you ask?'

Maz chimed in. 'A bit of trouble on the McKenzie farm, Wendy. Still early days, though. Once we know more, you will be the first to know.'

Smart by her, he thought. Not wanting to divulge too much information this early or upset the elderly woman, he knew Maz also knew how a small town could gossip.

'No unusual cars or people in the last few days?' he asked.

'Nothing off the top of my head,' she said, sipping from her cup of tea. 'Johns in town. I will ask him when he's home, though.'

'Sounds good. One last thing, do you know what he does for work?' he asked.

'He's a private investigator, from what I hear. He must be very busy. There always seems to be cars coming and going from his house. Come to think of it, it's odd that I haven't seen any cars over the last few days. I just assumed he was away for work.'

Nick sat and listened, and his mind raced with thoughts past this conversation, as he imagined the future of this investigation. Something didn't feel right here. He just couldn't put his finger on it yet.

'And he's never been over here before?' Maz asked.

'Actually yes, he has been here before, only the once. I was away on a trip with friends, but John told me about it when I got home, very unusual. He came over with a tape recorder and wanted to ask John about Belle Smith.'

The two officers slid forward on the couch at the same time. Curiosity now piqued, Nick asked, 'And what exactly did he want to know?'

'Well, John's the local doctor, officer, and the Smiths were patients at the surgery. I think he was asking John about their medical history.'

'Right, and what did John tell him?'

'Absolutely nothing. Patient doctor confidentiality is something that John holds very close. He told him to bugger off.'

'Fair enough,' Nick said, intrigued but slightly disappointed.

Getting back into Nick's car with a small plate of banana muffins covered in glad wrap, Maz looked in his direction. 'Really?'

'She wouldn't let me say no,' he replied sheepishly.

He started the car with a push of the button and headed down the driveway, indicating left towards the Smith's property. He was the first to break the silence. 'So, why was Harry McKenzie trying to get the medical information on the Smiths?'

'No idea. I'm guessing it has something to do with that board in his office, and this podcast business. Looks like he was trying to do our job for us. Finding out what happened to her.'

They continued down the small gravel road connecting the
three farms in quiet contemplation. It had now been a few
hours since they had found the body, and Nick knew he had
to call head office and update them on just what was going
on. He also knew that with ties to the Smith case, an absolute
media circus was going to descend onto Darfield, like one
that Maz had never seen, and not something the elderly
sergeant or her team would be prepared for. Once the news
got out, every man and their dog would have an opinion on
what connection this had to Belle's disappearance.

'I need to make a call,' he said.

'It's your car.'

After two short rings, the Chief Inspector answered. 'Nick,
how are ya, mate? You solved it yet?'

He looked across at Maz in the passenger seat, who had
her eyebrows raised.

'Unfortunately not, Chief. I'm calling with bad news.'

'Shit. I don't need this, Nick; I've got higher ups asking
me for updates every few days on this. What's wrong?'

'Looks like a murder, a local, Harry McKenzie is his
name.'

'A murder? Who is he? Any relation to what you're on?'

'He was actually a school friend of Belle's, as I understand. And looks to me like he was doing a bit of amateur sleuthing into her disappearance.'

'Jesus, we've got this podcast everywhere, and now locals are trying to solve this case as well. I'm sorry, but looks like you are going to be there a bit longer then, mate. I trust you can keep this between us for now? If the media gets a hold of this, it's going to be an absolute shit storm up there.'

'No worries Chief.'

Chapter Thirteen

Belle stood in the blazing sunlight and reached into the back tray of her uncle's ute to grab a bottle of water. The afternoon sun was at its peak in the sky and although it was a Saturday, she had promised her Dad and uncle she would give them a hand to mend the fencing across the back of the farm.

'Chuck us those wire cutters, would ya love?' Arthur said.

She grabbed the wire cutters from the tray and walked over to the section of fence where her Dad and uncle were working.

'Thanks.'

Using the cutters, Arthur expertly wove the new strand of fencing around the last new post that they had just put in the ground and ran his eye along the fence line with a smile. 'Couldn't get much better if ya' tried.'

'Nice work Art,' Tom said. 'How's school going, Belle?'

'Yeah, pretty good. Miss Jones gave me an A on my English exam, so can't complain about that.'

'Jesus, she still teaching up there? She must be a hundred years old!' he said with a chuckle.

Belle laughed along. 'Ninety-nine, I reckon.'

Belle walked back towards the shade of an enormous gum tree, which stood along the fence line. Her encounter with Harry McKenzie the other day at work had begun to eat at her, and she was more and more sure that he wasn't there for any other reason than just to watch her. It creeped her out, and she wanted to say something to her Dad, but was scared what his reaction might be. She had heard from people in town that her Dad was a criminal back in the day, which she found laughable. He was the sweetest and kindest person she had ever met. She knew he had a bit of a temper sometimes though and had seen him in some of his moods. Might be best to keep it to herself, she thought.

'You all right Bee?'

Tom had noticed Belle sitting in the shade of the gum tree, staring out into the distance. Walking over in her direction, he sat and offered her the last sandwich out of his esky.

'Yeah, I'm all right,' she said, continuing to look out ahead. She wanted to tell him how she was feeling, and although she trusted him, was unsure of how to proceed.

'Something bugging you, mate? You know you can talk to me whenever you need.'

She decided to just tell him. Surely, he could keep it to himself. 'There's a boy from school,' she said.

She sensed her uncle slightly stiffen beside her. And wondered whether maybe she shouldn't say any more. Maybe she should talk to her Mum about it instead? 'Go on,' he replied.

'His name is Harry McKenzie. He's in the year below me. I'm pretty sure he's got the hots for me.'

'Does he now? And how do you know that?'

'Well, I've noticed him watching me at school, and then the other week when I was at work, I found him watching me from the garden. I told him to bugger off, but honestly, it's given me the creeps.'

She watched as her uncle took a swig from his oversized water bottle. The afternoon sun had slowly begun to set on the horizon, the heat of the day now slowly leaving. She heard her Dad's four-wheeler motorbike start up from behind them and thought that may have been the end of their conversation.

'Well, no boy should be watching you like that, Bee. That's not right. McKenzie? Is that Alf's young fella?'

'Yeah, I think that's his Dad.'

Right, well, I might have a word with hi..'

Belle was mortified. 'No! don't please! I'll deal with it. I'll talk to him in the next few days. I'm sorry you don't need to be worrying about my stuff. I'm fine.'

'Are you sure? You know if you ever need me, just give me a shout, yeah?'

'Yeah. Thanks.'

Later that night, Tom sat at the end barstool in the Darfield hotel, sipping a cold pot of beer. He was worn out after the long day of fencing in the hot sun and felt the alcohol going to his head. He looked along the row of men perched up, listening to Dan Rogers talk about the latest giant fish he had caught. He thought the local publican was full of shit, but his missus was a local copper and he knew it was always better to be on the good side of local law enforcement, even if he hated the pigs.

He thought back to his earlier conversation with Belle and her troubles with the young McKenzie boy. It was starting; he thought to himself; she was becoming a woman before his eyes, and a good-looking one at that too, he had to admit. It was a shame her friend Anna was a bit on the plumper side, but thought she'd still be a good time if he had a crack.

Growing up, Arthur, his stepbrother, had tried his best to keep him out of trouble when they moved to Melbourne, but he was soon caught up in similar dramas to his older brother. 'I don't give a shit what you get involved in, Tom,' Arthur had said. 'But stay away from the gear. Shit's poison and I don't want it near our house.'

He had listened for a while, but the money that his friends were making dealing was soon too good to refuse. Slowly earning the trust of people in that world, he began to make his way up the chain and was soon one of the most sought-after dealers from the suburbs to the thriving city centre back then. It had all been too good to be true, of course, and when his brother got tied up in the Zimmer kidnapping, he tucked his tail between his legs and headed back for Mildura. He had decided to stay in Melbourne, but the coppers were clamping down on his trade and after a bar fight at his local pub in Port Melbourne, Arthur personally drove from Mildura to bail him out. Appreciative of the help, he too decided to head back home, in search of a simpler, trouble free life.

He drained the last of his pot and held his finger up for another. Walking around the main bar, he looked towards the old restaurant. There was a table of five women, all laughing and chatting, and sipping drinks from colourful glasses. He was in his forties now and had managed to keep in half decent shape through years of hard work on the farm, but he wasn't the young man he was back in his days in Melbourne. But he still knew how to talk to women and had one thing most of them couldn't refuse.

Standing in the toilet cubicle, he spread a neat white line of powder on top of the dirty toilet cistern. Rolling up a twenty-dollar note, he snorted the fine powder and rubbed his left nostril, feeling his eyes water. This shit was good and getting better, he thought. Better not have too much too early. Who knows who I might be sharing it with later with those girls around?

After three more beers, he was starting to feel the effects of the drugs beginning to wear off, and thought he might need to head to the bathroom for another hit when he noticed Alf McKenzie walk in. Remembering his conversation with Belle earlier, he made a beeline for the farmer. 'How are ya Alf?'

Alf looked over at Tom with a mixture of fear and curiosity. The Smiths' life of crime before coming to Darfield was well known, and his reputation proceeded him. Unsure of what he would want with him, he answered, 'Tom. Good mate, you?'

'Yeah, yeah, busy as always. Hey, ya mind if we have a word?'

Alf looked at Tom and could tell by his eyes that he was on something and didn't want to say the wrong thing to offend. His older brother was known to have a bad temper, and he wasn't sure if Tom had the same. He hoped it was something to do with their farm; he wasn't much of a farmer, which was well known throughout the town, but was always happy to help those in need if he could.

'Of course,' he said, as Tom ushered him over towards the end of the bar, out of earshot of the other patrons.

Keeping his voice barely above a whisper, in a menacing tone Alf hadn't heard before, he looked over towards the bar and then back towards him. 'You keep your son away from my niece. If I hear from her he's hanging around again, I'll kill him.

Chapter Fourteen

Nick's phoned chimed as he turned through the gates of Belgrove, the Smith's farm. A text from Bec popped up on his screen. 'We've got something here. You need to see this.'

Already halfway down the driveway, he tapped a quick reply. 'Heading to the Smiths, won't be long.' Whatever it was, it would have to wait.

The long gravel driveway snaked around a small dam which was in front of what looked to be a thriving vegetable garden. Redgum sleepers were stacked in neat rectangles, forming around eight separate garden beds.

'That's where the house used to be,' Maz said, pointing out at the garden.

Looking back at the dam, he asked, 'And I take it that's the famous dam I've heard so much about?'

'Yep, that's it.'

Heading past the vegetable garden, they came up on a small beige single storey home with another wraparound veranda. The porch had metal handrailing around it, still unpainted in a fading zinc colour, with the welds on each join at the posts now rusted. The home was of very similar styling to the Sexton's and the McKenzie's; he thought to himself, and he soon realised that most of these homes must be of been rebuilt by the same builder after the fires. To lose your entire home and all of its contents must have been devastating, he thought, but nothing could be as bad as losing your child. As he looked around at the property that he had read and listen so much about, the disappearance of Belle Smith suddenly felt much more real and present as he stood on their property. And the reason he was here in Darfield in the first place.

'Help you?' came a voice from behind him, walking out of the machinery shed.

Nick turned around and looked over in the voice's direction. A now much older Arthur Smith stood before him. Wearing torn work jeans, and a faded green zip up jumper, he had aged a lot since the last picture he had seen of him and now walked with a slight stoop. His hair was thinning across the top of his head, with the fine grey strands spread across his sun spotted scalp.

'Detective Nick Vada,' he said, with his hand outstretched.

Giving it a firm shake, Arthur replied, 'Arthur Smith, people call me Art.'

'Thanks Art, and I'm sure you know Sergeant Rogers?'

'I do. Hi Maz. I wondered when you would be coming out here.'

'Oh? Whys that?'

'Heard a detective was in town. Sniffing around about us.'

'Well, you're right there. I was sent out to investigate your daughter's disappearance, which I'd like to chat with you and your wife about in due time. However, it seems like there has been a bit of trouble over at McKenzie farm.'

Art's demeanour seemed to soften, at ease now he didn't need to speak about his lost daughter for the next few minutes. 'At Harry's? What happened?'

Maz chimed in, 'Nothing we can speak about as yet. Art, have you seen or heard anything from there over the last few days?'

Art scratched the stubble on his chin, lost in thought. 'I saw a Landcruiser work ute heading down the driveway that I

haven't seen before the other day, gathered it was a Roo
shooter going by the gunshots.'

Nick and Maz looked at each other. 'Gunshots?'

'Yeah, two days ago, I heard maybe four shots. Assumed
it was a Roo shooter. Harry's not much of a shooter himself.
He'd asked Tom if he could come over and get rid of a couple
that were damaging his fences the other month. I guessed
he'd just hired someone in for it.'

'You didn't happen to get a registration on the ute?' he
asked.

Arthur scoffed. 'Shit, you think I have binoculars to spy
on my neighbours? Only reason I saw it was because I was
out weeding the veggie garden, it was a white Landcruiser,
with a steel tray. That's all I can tell you.'

Nick jotted notes quickly in his notepad and knew his first
point of call after they went back to the McKenzie's would be
to put out an APB for everyone to be on the lookout for the
white ute.

'Thanks Art, very helpful,' Maz replied. 'Is Ness in?'

'Sure, she's inside.'

Heading back over towards the house, he noted that
although in poor condition on the outside; it was still quite

neat and tidy. Growing up in the bush himself, he had seen many farms and knew that during busy periods, the house was the last thing the families would attend to after a day out on the land. The wraparound veranda had decking that was well maintained and looked like recently had just another coat of oil applied. Two old chairs sat underneath a window with a side table in between them that had a pile of paperback novels on them, and two drink coasters on either side.

Maz knocked on the security door, and they soon heard footsteps heading toward them. Opening the door, Vanessa Smith looked at the two officers with a mixture of curiosity and sadness. She had aged much better than Art he thought, Slim with dark jeans on and a blue and white striped button-up shirt, she was attractive for her age and didn't look a day older than the 60 minutes interview he had seen recently, which was from ten years earlier. Her hair was tied up in a loose bun and was a dark brown, with light streaks of grey throughout. She must have been in her late fifties to early sixties, he assumed, but could still pass for someone much younger.

'Maz, how are you, love?'

'I'm good thanks, Ness, this is Detective Sergeant Nick Vada, hoping we could ask you a couple of questions.'

Nick smiled in her direction and held out his hand. 'I wondered when I'd be seeing you,' she replied.

'I'd planned on coming out to chat about your daughter, Mrs. Smith, but there has been a bit of trouble over at the McKenzie property.'

Vanessa looked in the direction of the McKenzie farm. 'At Harry's? What's wrong?'

'We'll let you know more soon, but right now we'd just like to know if you had seen or heard anything out of the ordinary from over there?'

'Nothing off the top of my head. Art said he'd heard someone shooting Roo's the other day, but that's about it?'

He looked over Ness's shoulder into their lounge room as she spoke. He saw that above their fireplace on the mantlepiece was a small shrine of photographs of their daughter Belle.

'May I?' he asked, pointing over at the photos.

'Go ahead.'

He walked through the lounge room and looked over the various photos of Belle throughout her life. Baby photos, her first steps, a picture of her playing sport, and a picture of her and Anna Denholm, probably very close to the time before she went missing.

As he studied the photo of the two girls closely, Ness answered the question on his mind. 'That was about two months before she went missing,' she said.

Nick thought about Harry's murder, and the Smith family, and their years of loss and grief. The text from Bec would have to wait. He was going to sit down with Vanessa and hear her story.

He looked at photos of Joe, their youngest, beside Belle, and asked, 'Where's your son these days?'

Vanessa sighed, 'Western Australia. He went over to the mines a few years ago. We don't see much of him anymore. Losing his sister was a big shock back then. I'm not sure if he ever got over it.'

'I can't even imagine. Look, I was sent here from Sydney to have a look at your daughter's disappearance, Mrs. Smith. I'm a detective with the homicide special investigations unit. I'm originally from Milford, and I think they assume that my time in the bush and my rural experience may help in some way.

'I've read about you in the paper, detective. I think it may be a bit more than that. You solved a double homicide in your hometown last year, and your own mother's cold case murder.'

He wasn't surprised she knew about him solving the double homicide in his hometown, due to it being spread across news coverage and papers for the next month. But solving his mother's murder was something that was kept within the police. He had asked his Chief Inspector to try to keep it as quiet as possible and was glad that the media had not gotten a hold of it. It was a chapter in his life he wanted to leave behind.

'How did you know about my mother's murder?' he asked.

'I have been searching for my daughter's murderer for 23 years, detective. I have trawled every local newspaper, website, message board, social media group, and any case files under the Freedom of Information Act that I could, in search of something, anything, that could help in finding what happened to her. I remember reading of your mother's death years ago when I was reading a true crime book on Jim Hooper's story and put two and two together when I heard it had been solved.'

'Fair enough. Look, I can tell you have obviously left no stone unturned, and it's my job now to start from the beginning, pull this thing apart and try to find any inconsistencies.'

Vanessa smiled at that. 'Let me boil the kettle and make us all a cuppa. Please, take a seat.'

As the two officers sat down in the dining room, he felt his phone vibrate once again in his pocket. 'You sure we have time for this?' Maz asked him quietly.

'McKenzie isn't going anywhere. I'm sure Bec and Neville are on top of it for now. We won't be long.'

He could tell she was frustrated by her body language and knew she had probably heard this story a million times over by now. But he knew sometimes all it took was a fresh set of eyes to turn the whole thing upside down. As Vanessa sat down at the dining table, she sipped from her cup of tea and looked expectantly in Nick's direction. He pulled his phone and silenced it, turning on his recorder app in the process.

'From the beginning,' he said.

Chapter Fifteen

Vanessa looked down at her cup of tea and began, 'It was an absolutely scorching day. We were used to the heat, but it was relentless that summer. The wind that morning just seemed to slowly build, stronger and stronger. We had kept up with the reports of bushfires, but we had never had anything come close to the farm before. I had heard stories on the TV of people who at the last minute had lost everything, and who had wished they were better prepared. I spoke with Art that night and he decided I should head into town early and buy extra hoses for the water pump just in case we needed to put out any grass fires.'

'So, what time did you leave that morning?'

'Early. Joe was off school, and I knew Belle would be okay at home with Art. Believe me, it's something that has eaten at me for all these years since. Why didn't I bring her along?'

Nick knew that the family of missing children often lived with years of regret and grief, stewing over tiny moments in the days leading up to their disappearances, thinking of ways they could have changed the outcome.

'I got stuck in town. I ended up helping Val Collins load up her wagon with supplies for their horse stables. By the time I got back out to the farm, the weather had worsened, and pretty much as soon as I got there, the fire was on our back doorstep.'

'And where were Arthur and Tom during all of this?'

'Art was filling all the spare water tanks. He was going to fill all the gutters around the house and sheds. He'd spent the day before slashing the grass around the house, but hadn't got to the shed yet. That's how it got to the house. The shed went first and the house next. Tom turned up just in front of the fire. It had skirted around his place at the property, luckily, but when the wind changed, it headed straight for us.'

He could imagine the stress running through the family the day of the fires and knew it would have been easy to assume Belle had simply stayed in town, with the severity of the fires not known until it was right on top of them. He imagined the Smiths had been so busy in the rush to protect their property that they wouldn't have had time for concern just yet.

'So, you didn't see Belle that morning?'

'No, I didn't. Art was out early as well, but swears he thought he saw her on the way to the bathroom to get ready for school. He's gone back and forwards on it a few times, but I still believe he saw her.'

'So, when did you start to worry?'

'I tried to call the house phone when I was in town on my mobile, to see if Art needed anything else, when no one answered I called the school to check if Belle was there, but it rang and rang and they never answered.' She took another sip of her tea and continued, 'By the time I got back, I was a bit of a mess. The school wasn't answering. Anna hadn't seen her, so I really started to worry. I actually spoke with Maz that day on the phone.'

Maz chimed in. 'I remember it like it was yesterday. It was a madhouse. We were getting calls from all directions. The fire was coming for the town, and we were trying our best to clear out the properties in town. It moved so quickly, we just hoped that the farmers would do their best to fight it off.'

'I let Maz know that we couldn't find her, and she let me know they would try their best to get out to the farm and take down some info. That was just before the fire hit.'

He sat in silence, listening to the clearly still grieving mother talk. He too had lost a family member, his mother, at a young age. The grief came in waves. Sometimes he could go months without even thinking about it and then a thought would pop into his head, and he couldn't get it out of his head for the rest of the day.

'So, I know you've probably been asked this a million times before, but was there anything unusual about Belle over the last few months leading to her disappearance?'

The clock in the dining room ticked loudly over the silence between the trio, and Vanessa sipped from her tea again. 'As I've said before nothing really, I felt she was a bit quieter in the last few weeks, and she spent a lot more time in her bedroom with the door closed, but I just chalked that up to the fact that she was a teenage girl, and she wanted her privacy.'

Over in the kitchen, the sliding door opened, and Tom Smith walked over the threshold. 'Hey Ness, Art said you got the keys to the..' He stopped in his tracks at the sight of three sitting at the dining room table.

Nick looked over at the younger Smith brother. Without the stoop, he was taller than Art. He still had a head full of hair, and it was still a dark brown with small flecks of grey.

He was more of a mystery to Nick, not mentioned much in the case file, or on the podcast so far. He hadn't yet got a read on him.

'Hi Tom, keys are on the bench,' she said.

Tom eyed the two police officers with suspicion and removed his thick farming gloves and made his way over to the trio. 'What's this all about, then?'

'Detective Vada,' Nick said as he held out his hand.

Tom looked at his hand for a second, and didn't return the handshake. He looked directly at him and asked, 'Is this about Belle?'

Nick had imagined the family may have a distrust of the police, but so far, it was only Tom who seemed to rub him the wrong way. From the minute he walked into the room, his senses were set alight as he looked at him. 'It is, Tom I assume?' he said.

'Yeah, who wants to know?'

Sensing the tension in the room, Vanessa said, 'This is Tom, detective, Belle's uncle. Tom was very close to Belle. They were inseparable when she was a little girl. He was like a second father to her.'

Nick wondered why there wasn't more information about him in the case file. Being so close to Belle, surely he would have been an invaluable resource for the police back then. 'Just talking with Mrs. Smith about the days leading up to Belle's disappearance.'

'What about it?'

'Had you noticed anything unusual about her?'

'Nah, nothing at all.'

He felt like this conversation wasn't going to go anywhere with Tom still in the room and could feel the man's resentment toward them. Feeling like the progress he was making talking to Vanessa diminishing, he decided to cut their chat short and head back to the McKenzie property.

He cleared his throat. 'Right then, I think that will be all for now. Thanks, Vanessa, we've got to get going.'

Tom stood awkwardly at the kitchen's entrance, and he felt like there were words unspoken by the man. 'Actually, there was one thing I suppose I didn't really talk about then,' he said.

Vanessa sat up straighter in her chair, now keen to hear more. 'What Tom?'

He looked down at the ground as he spoke. 'Young Harry McKenzie. He was bothering Bee. She told me a couple of weeks before she went missing. I bailed up Alf McKenzie in the pub though, and I sorted it out, Ness.'

Vanessa's face turned red and her eyes welled with tears. 'Wait, what are you saying? All of this time! Why didn't you say anything earlier?!'

Tom looked extremely uncomfortable now. 'You know I hate the coppers, Ness; I never spoke to em' back then. They never asked me.'

Knowing that Harry McKenzie lay dead in a paddock a few kilometres away, this information changed things dramatically.

'How was he bothering her?' Maz asked.

Tom shrugged. 'Following her around, watching her at work. I just guessed he had a thing for her. You know how young fellas are.'

'Watching her!' Vanessa yelled. 'Tom! You should've told me!'

Maz, sensing the conversation between the two family members beginning to worsen, stepped in to calm them both down. 'Vanessa, why don't we head outside, and Nick can finish up with Tom?'

Vanessa looked over at her brother-in-law. Her makeup had started to run, and he knew that when they left, there was going to be hell to pay. Why hadn't the younger Smith brother spoken to the police? He knew there must be history there. But was it seriously enough to not aid in finding your lost niece?

When the two women had left the room, he noticed the elderly farmer stand up straighter, bringing himself to his full height. He was slightly shorter than Nick, but he could tell the man had lived a hard life on the land and noticed deep scars across his knuckles and forearms, all with their own stories, of a different time.

He broke the silence. 'So, Harry McKenzie is next door, right now, lying dead in his back paddock. You know anything about that?'

He hoped the brutal honesty might knock the guy down a peg. Tom's mouth opened and his eyes were wide with shock. 'D-Dead? What do you mean? I only saw him the other day?'

'Shot. From close range, going by the wound,' Nick continued, 'And Art tells me you've done a bit of shooting on his property?'

He held his hands up. 'Whoa, I've got nothing to do with anything like that. You can ask Art and Ness. I've been on the farm since the weekend. We've been flat out prepping for seeding. Does Ness know?'

'No, I haven't told her.'

'Shit. She's going to be upset. He was over here a bit. I think they were trying to figure out what happened to Belle together.'

Nick was perplexed. 'And you never thought to tell her what had happened with Harry back then?'

'I honestly didn't think it had anything to do with it. If he was so guilty, why did he use to spend all his time with Ness trying to find her killer?'

'Who said she was killed? This is a missing person's case,' Nick interjected.

'That's just my opinion.'

'And why did you say used to spend his time?'

Tom looked blankly back at him. 'He and Ness had a falling out. I'd rather not go into it.'

Nick looked the man in the eyes and had a bad feeling about him. He had to get back to McKenzie's, but Tom Smith was a new name on his radar.

'Fair enough.' He handed his card over to him, which Tom threw back onto the dining table. 'You have anything else to tell me. Make sure you call me.'

'Yeah, nah, I think I'll be right.'

Chapter Sixteen

Nick and Maz headed back towards the McKenzie farm, both lost in thought. Rolling the information about McKenzie in his head, he was left with more questions than answers. Why didn't Tom Smith tell his brother or sister-in-law about McKenzie hanging around Belle? Seemed like a pretty important piece to the puzzle. There was something off about the guy which rubbed him the wrong way. 'What's this Tom Smith's deal? Has he caused you any drama over the years?'

Maz shrugged. 'Not a peep. Drinks in the pub sometimes, pleasant enough fellow. Rumour has it back in the day that he ran with a rough crowd, back when he was in Melbourne. But from as far as I'm concerned, he hasn't caused me any trouble.'

'Well, he doesn't like police, that's for sure. I thought he was going to take a swing at me for a minute there.'

The sun was beginning to lower in the sky as they turned back down McKenzie's driveway and the rain had eased, causing steam to rise from the warm sand on the road leading to the house.

'I just don't understand why he wouldn't have told his brother,' Maz said.

'Like he said, he didn't think it had anything to do with it. I don't believe a word out of his mouth, though. I think we need to dig a bit deeper into that and ask around. It's a shame we couldn't ask Alf McKenzie about it.'

'And this falling out with Ness? What do you think that's about?' Maz asked.

'That's easy.' He had thought about it more. Harry had accused Art Smith of murdering Belle on the podcast. That would have been enough to cause a massive rift between the two. 'The podcast. He accused Art Smith of killing Belle.'

'God, I'm stupid, I didn't think. That would explain it.'

The lone shed behind the McKenzie household was now a hive of activity. The white crime scene services van was flanked by two of the local police vehicles and a black coroner's van was nudged in the end of the row. Tall lighting towers had been set up on either end of the shed, with one shining into the old building and one shining out into the paddock, illuminating the farm as the sun began to set.

As they got out of the car, Bec walked over in their direction. She had a pair of white medical gloves on, and her dark blue uniform was covered in dust and cobwebs.

'You look like you've been busy,' he said.

'Very. We were lucky. Stan, our forensic pathologist, lives halfway between Mildura and Darfield. He came as soon as I called.'

They walked over towards the entrance to the shed and under the two white gazebos that had been setup and multiple pieces of evidence were spread across the tables underneath. Looking over the items on the tables, he found a plastic clip-lock bag with three shell casings, a cigarette butt, and a bloody piece of rag. Looking over at the next table, a lone wooden crate sat on it, covered in oil and cobwebs. As he went to walk over towards it, Bec yelled out his name. 'Nick, over here!'

He walked back out towards the crime scene, towards the group of people illuminated under the floodlight. Night had now begun to set, and he could feel his stomach rumbling, the banana muffin feeling like it was days ago.

The elderly forensic pathologist stood before him in jeans and a black navy zip up jumper. He looked to be in his early 60s with a bulging stomach and a beetroot red nose. The man

was a heavy drinker, that was for sure. 'Evening detective.
Dr. Stan Hathaway.'

'Evening Doc, thanks for coming out so late. What have
you got?'

Kneeling beside the body, the doctor pointed at his chest.
'One gunshot wound to the chest. He was shot in the back.
The bullet continued through and ended up in the tree line out
there.'

Neville spoke up from beside him. 'We've started a search
out there, but it's too dark, and the rain hasn't done us any
favours. We'll continue tomorrow.'

Bec added, 'It will help us confirm exactly how many
shots were made. I'm sure you saw on the table, we found
bullet shells.'

'Looked like 308 casings?' he asked.

'Spot on, a very common bullet around these parts. I'd
hazard a guess to say nearly every farm out here would use
something similar. We'll send them off to the lab for analysis,
but that'll take time.'

He knew most farmers had a standard array of firearms on
their property and that a 308 bullet could be used in a
multitude of rifles. Narrowing down to the exact model could

help and they could cross check with local and surrounding gun shops to see if they could find a match.

'Where'd you find them?' Maz asked.

'By the back door of the house, looks like you guys had walked right by them.'

Nick walked back away from the group, and the four followed. As he got back to the rear door of the house, he turned back around and faced them, holding a mock rifle in his hand in a shooting position, out into the paddock to where Harry had fallen. 'It's around one hundred and fifty metres, so we are looking for a scoped weapon. And someone who was an excellent shot,' he said to the group.

He imagined Harry sitting in the lounge room, seeing a vehicle come down his driveway. Getting up to see who it is, he sees a figure emerge from the vehicle with a rifle. Perhaps already sensing his fate, he breaks into a run, straight out his back door. He aims for the cover of the machinery shed. With three sharp pops, bullets fizz menacingly through the air around him as he cries out for help. With the last bullet entering his back, he falls forward in his paddock. The shooter hasn't even stepped off his back deck, and turns straight back around and comes out the way they came in.

'Maz, tomorrow morning, get Pat or Sam to check over the National Gun Register. Most of the guns in the region should be on it.'

'Will do. Look, my guys have been out here all day. I might knock one of them off if you don't mind?'

'Fine by me.'

She walked off over in the direction of the two younger officers, who looked to be searching through the old work shed. The rain had begun to fall again, and a fine mist was now making the group wet. He could feel the rain taking its toll on the group and knew they weren't going to achieve anything further out there tonight in these conditions.

'I'm going to get him packed up and out of here,' Stan said.

He watched as the forensic examiner and two crime scene officers packed the body into a black body bag and walked off on a stretcher. The farm no longer had an owner, and poor Bailey no longer had a Dad.

Bec returned after seeing the pathologist off. She looked worn out, and he could tell the conditions had taken their toll and the day had finally caught up with her.

'Are you ok? You look beat,' he asked.

She sighed. 'It's been a long day. This weather is killing us out here, we're going to lose so much potential evidence. Looks like we are going to be here for a while.'

'You rang earlier?'

She smiled. 'I did. I think I might have something to help with the other case you are working on. Follow me.'

They walked back underneath the gazebo and looked over the tables covered in evidence and investigation gear. 'What am I looking at?' he asked.

'There's a smaller shed which comes off the back-left corner of this main building. Inside it was a small tool shop. Looked to me like it hadn't had much use over the years.'

'Go on.'

'I found that crate,' she said, pointing to the small box on the further table.

The rain had intensified as Nick made his way over to the second table, with the steady patter falling on the two quick shade gazebos. He looked at the box and wondered just what was so interesting about it. It looked like the same crates his fathers had used in his own tool shed, to store tools and other junk.

'Look inside,' Bec said.

He came closer to the box and leaned his face over the opening. There, covered in dust and cobwebs, was a neatly folded Darfield High School dress, with 'Class of 2000' embroidered over the pocket.

Chapter Seventeen

Nick stood still, staring into the old crate in a mixture of shock and disbelief.

'Do you think this is Belle's?'

'We don't know for sure. We will test for DNA if we can get a sample from the Smith family, but it can't be a coincidence. Weren't there only like five other girls in that class?'

His mind raced with possibilities; they could be a lot closer to some answers than he thought. 'You sound like you've been doing your research.'

'I've read a lot about this case. It was absolutely everywhere when I was growing up. I always assumed she was lost in the fire until I listened to the podcast. Now it looks like there may be more to the story going by this.'

He knew the timeline like the back of his hand and tried to line up how and why Belle Smith's school uniform would be in Harry McKenzie's possession. It seemed like McKenzie was obsessed with the case, going by his home office and the podcast interview. But why would he have a crucial piece of evidence stashed in the shed behind his house? Was it some kind of sick memento?

Bec carefully removed the folded dress from the crate and placed it into a large evidence bag. As he watched her, he felt waves of fatigue; the action filled day finally catching up with him. He looked out of the gazebo and realised everyone else had left except for Pat, the young officer, who was watching them intently.

'Are you sticking around, Pat?' he asked.

'Maz has me keeping an eye on things out here. Sam will come out and take over a bit later.'

'Did she take Bailey in?'

'Yep, she's taking her back to the pub.'

'Thanks, mate, I know it's thankless work, but you're a key part of this team and investigation.'

The young officer swelled with pride and puffed his chest slightly out at the comment. He knew a sprinkling of compliments always helped when morale was low.

'Thanks, Detective,' he said with a smile.

He turned back to Bec and mustered up the courage to ask the next question, as it had been on his mind the minute he laid eyes on her. 'Are you sticking around? I'm starved. Pub for dinner?'

They sat in the cosy warm bistro at the Darfield Hotel and eyed the menus. He noticed she had put a lip gloss on her lips on the drive over, and they glistened in the light from overhead. She had changed from her navy-blue police uniform into dark jeans and a pale blue button up polo shirt. Her hair was tied up in a messy bun and he was sure she was the prettiest woman to have ever stepped foot in that pub. He looked down at his dirty chinos and button-up shirt and tried to brush off a piece of cobweb from the shed on his shoulder, annoyed he hadn't freshened up a bit more before they met to eat.

She placed the menu down on the table and smiled. 'Well, it's pretty much the same menu every pub in the state has, so I'm pretty sure I know what I'll order.'

As she finished, a young waitress walked past with two plates balanced on her left arm. Two huge burgers the size of small footballs were placed down on the table beside them, in front of two hungry men in fluoro yellow work shirts.

'I think I'll get a steak,' he said.

After ordering together, they made their way back to their small table with drinks in hand. He didn't feel like a drink but didn't want to be rude when Bec ordered wine. He sipped the cold beer and felt the cool liquid fizz down his throat, immediately feeling lighter as the alcohol hit his system.

'So, are you seeing anyone?' she asked.

Nick's love life had been pretty bleak over the last few years. He had had an on-again-off-again relationship with a real estate agent in the city that ended abruptly a few years back. In more recent times, he had rekindled a childhood romance with a girl from his hometown. They had tried to make it work over a long distance, but it soon fizzled out, another wasted opportunity.

'Wow. Straight to the point. No, I'm not, not a lot of time for romance in this job. You?'

'Same for me. By the time I work, study, and spend time with my nieces and nephews, there's not a lot of time for romance in the Ranijan household.'

'What are you studying?'

'A doctorate in forensic science. I finished my masters years ago and after a while, I thought it's only another three years. Why not become Dr Bec Ranijan?'

'Yeah, why not?' He was impressed. He could tell she was a woman who didn't rest on her laurels and strived to be better.

Once they had finished their meals, they sat and discussed life, with Nick filling her in on all the details of his last few cases, and his time in his hometown when they first met. Watching her laugh, he felt an ease around her and was comfortable in confiding his feelings about the time and the emotions that revolved around solving his own mother's murder.

She sipped her wine with a smile. 'So, the million-dollar question is, why didn't you ever call me?'

Nick nearly choked on his drink. Feeling his face go red, he decided that the truth was the best option. 'Look at you, Bec, you're stunning. I felt like you were way out of my league.'

Nick watched her smile spread slowly over her face and right up to her eyes. 'Don't sell yourself short Nick, you have a very low opinion of yourself, don't you? Have you seen how the others were looking at you today? You're a brilliant investigator and a natural-born leader.'

'I appreciate that.'

'It's fine. And also, you're not too bad looking yourself.'

He could feel now how hot his face was and decided to change the subject. He looked down at his watch and realised the time. 'It's getting late. We have a big day tomorrow.'

Bec knew the detective couldn't take any form of a compliment. 'I agree. I'm headed back out to Stan's for the night. Will I see you back on the farm tomorrow?'

He nodded. 'I'll do my best; I'm going to take Maz and head back to Belgrove. I'd like to take a statement from Tom Smith and speak further with Arthur and Vanessa Smith.'

He walked Bec out of the small pub and into the moonlit night. She pulled her keys out of her pocket, unlocked the white police van, and turned back in his direction. With a swift step towards him which caught him off guard, she stood on tippy toes and planted her lips on his, and he felt Darfield, the murders, and Belle's disappearance, all slip away for a brief moment.

'Goodnight Nick.'

'Night, Bec,' he replied, still a little shocked.

Waving her van off, he stood in the car park, unable to wipe the smile off his face. He hadn't forgotten about her from the moment they met, and seeing her again was a welcome surprise.

After having a quick shower in the communal blocks at the back of the pub, he sat at the table beside the kitchenette in his caravan and read through his emails. Hearing a knock at the door, he walked over and opened it.

Standing at the entrance was Dan Rogers, holding a leash with Bailey connected to it. She sat expectantly with her tail wagging, looking up at Nick with what he thought looked like her best smile.

'Pat dropped her off before. Looks like she'll be staying for a few nights?'

'If that's okay with you, mate?'

Dan gave her a scratch on the head. 'Of course, we lost our old girl, Molly, only a couple of years ago. I've been telling Maz we need another dog around here to keep us company.'

He handed the lead over to Nick and he unclipped it. She had a quick shake and made her way inside. 'Go on, make yourself at home, girl.'

Bailey padded over and jumped up on the end of his bed, and after a quick stretch, she fell into a deep sleep. He sat back down at the table and watched the old dog sleep peacefully. One of her eyes was only half closed, and soon she was rhythmically letting out quiet snores. He wished he could ask her what she had seen. She probably had all the answers that he needed at that moment.

Looking back at his phone, he was surprised to see one notification from his podcast app. Curious, he swiped it open and read the blurb beneath the new 'special update' episode of Into The Flames. Surely it wasn't what he thought it was. There's no way news could travel that fast. He grabbed his phone and lay down on the old bed beside Bailey. He stretched out and lay the mobile down beside his head and pressed play, and listened in.

'Good evening, my name is Prue Thornton, and I am your host of Into The Flames. It's late afternoon here in rainy Melbourne, but I have just been told some devastating news. Unfortunately, Harry McKenzie, a long-time collaborator, and friend, has been found dead on his property a short time ago. Details are still scarce on the ground and I do not want to start any rumours before the police have time to investigate, but I believe it may have been foul play.'

Nick paused the phone and sat up quickly. He forwarded the episode link straight to Maz Rogers. How the hell did it get out so quick? Either someone involved in the investigation on the farm today had told this Prue Thornton, or one of the Smiths had spoken to her. There wasn't anyone else who knew that McKenzie was dead.

He could feel a storm brewing, and knew when his Chief found out about this, he was going to cop a barrage of questions. He pressed play again and continued to listen.

'I am personally making the trip up to Darfield tomorrow, and will report further when I am on the ground. We all here at Into The Flames have had our suspicions about certain suspects in this famous case and we hope the police listen to us and look further into what we have discovered. We will all grieve for Harry, and he will be forever in our hearts. We will stop at nothing to get justice for his death, whether it was an accident or not. Stay tuned for the next episode this week.'

He threw his phone down onto the bed in frustration. Whoever had told Prue Thornton the news had seriously jeopardised his investigation, and he knew it was about to become an absolute circus in the small town. He needed to get in front of it before it arrived and find some answers. The disappearance needed to go on the back burner for now, and he needed to find out just who killed Harry McKenzie.

Chapter Eighteen

Nick sat in the Police station the next day on one side of Maz Rogers' desk with the old witness statements and photographs from the days of Belle Smith's disappearance spread across it. Maz had a cigarette hanging out of her mouth, and a half-full cup of coffee in her left hand. She looked stressed and he could tell that she knew the town was about to be inundated now the news was out, and he wondered how she was going to handle it.

'I just don't understand how she found out. Pat and Sam are kids. They wouldn't have told a soul?'

'I think it was the Smiths,' he said.

'It's more likely them than one of us.'

Sam sat on the desk to the left-hand side of him, listening to them debate. 'Have either of you actually listened to the whole season of the podcast?'

'No, just the first two episodes,' he said.

'Vanessa Smith is interviewed in the final episode, and she speaks on the family's behalf. She fights for Arthur's innocence and swears that he had nothing to do with it. She believes that Belle was taken by someone.'

'Well, she's always going to stick up for her husband, I guess. That's a given. Looks like we need to work off the assumption that Vanessa Smith was the one that has told her about Harry.' Maz looked back towards Nick. 'What a shitshow. How do we get in front of this?'

He sat at the desk and scratched at the stubble on his chin. His mind was far away, currently back in the carpark still from the night before. As soon as he heard the podcast, he knew immediately that the Smiths had been the one to tell the host. He knew that the officers wouldn't have been stupid enough to leak information that sensitive and so quickly out; it was something more likely to of happen in the city, with the media having close contacts within the police. The family had been grieving now for many years, and with no leads, the podcast was the spark of hope that they needed and he knew that any new information they thought could help in finding their daughter would be spread as far and wide as they knew how and as fast as possible. It's exactly what he would have done if he was in the same position.

'I think I'll speak with our media liaison and get a news conference set up. We'll keep the details sparse, but it might be good to let everyone know where the investigation currently stands. We need to do our best to stay in front of it, and try to stop the rumour mill for now. How did we go with the APB for the white ute?'

Sam replied, 'I put it out late last night. I've sent it to all stations within a 500km radius. As soon as I hear anything, I will let you know.'

He was impressed at her speed. Getting it out last night was a huge help. Any hours extra were pivotal in an investigation like this and would aid them in finding the vehicle.

'Great work. I'd like you to head back out to the McKenzie farm and ask officer Ranijan if there's anything you can do to help. Maz and I will head back out to Belgrove for some further questioning. I'd like to speak with Tom Smith again. Maz, what do we know about Tom Smith?'

Maz sipped the last of her tea and placed her cigarette butt into the now empty mug with a hiss. 'Not a lot. Arthur's younger brother and Belle's only uncle. He works on the farm out there with them, and as far as I know, he's worked there ever since he moved out into his house. He lives out at the back of the farm in a small demountable home.'

'Was he interviewed when Belle first went missing?'

'Not that I remember. If it isn't in these files here, it didn't happen. I remember him being around the farm in the days after the fire. He and Arthur searched the property day and night for those first few nights. A small group of locals came out the first day to help out, but with no leads and nothing to go on, they slowly dwindled away. I know the Tom, the sergeant, back at the time spoke with him on and off, but he was never formally interviewed, to my knowledge.'

'Has he got a record?' Nick asked.

'Back in the 80s, he followed Art to Melbourne. We know what Art was involved in, so safe to assume he was tied up in it as well. His record shows petty thefts and small-time drug charges. When he got here to Darfield, nothing.'

The drugs were interesting to Nick as he knew reading Arthur's record there wasn't any mention of drug charges. Back in the 80s, it was a booming time for them in the major cities. After US soldiers brought heroin into the country during the Vietnam War, the drug trade in Melbourne and Sydney intensified, with rival gangs importing more and more of it. Marijuana was always popular, and methamphetamines became a popular drug for the younger crowds. If the Smiths were involved in drugs back then, what caused them to stop and move and back to Darfield? And what connections did this have with Belle's disappearance?

'What were the drug charges?'

'Marijuana possession, small quantities of methamphetamines, three separate times.'

'That is interesti..'

Halfway through his sentence, he heard the loud dinging of the bell on the counter from out in reception. Maz looked at him curiously and waved Sam off in its direction. 'See what that's about, love.'

She walked out of the room and off down the hallway. Minutes later, she came back and spoke in Nick's direction. 'She's asking for you.' Nick spun around and faced the young officer, who had a wide smile and continued, 'You're not going to believe it.'

He got up out of the chair and followed her back down the small police station's hallway, curious as to who even knew he was in Darfield beside the police. Standing at the front counter was a small Asian woman with dark black hair in a bob cut. Wearing dark jeans and a bright blue Nike jumper, she had her mobile phone placed on top of the counter, with an elaborate microphone attached to the top of it.

'Detective Nick Vada I'm guessing?'

'The one and only, and you are?'

She looked almost offended at the question. Slightly taken aback, she blinked and smiled. 'Prue Thornton, at your service.'

So, this was the famous Prue Thornton. After listening to the special update of Into The Flames, he quickly did some research into her career. Originally a journalist, she quickly worked her way up the ranks at the Herald Sun in Melbourne and finished her time as an investigative journalist. Pivoting at the right time, she started podcasting and was the first ever Walkley award recipient for her smash hit podcast, Dead Still, which had a rabid fanbase. Looking into the cold case of missing five-year-old boy Patrick Hamer, she managed to reignite the dormant case and get police back on the trail. Through an anonymous tip to the podcast and the help of her millions strong fanbase, fifty-four-year-old truck driver Simon Positano was arrested and charged for the little boys' abduction and murder, ending a family's fifteen-year quest for the police to look back into it.

'So how do I pronounce your last name? V-A-D-A? like Darth Vader from Star Wars?'

'Correct.' He had heard that more times than he could remember. 'It's nice to meet you, Miss Thornton. What can I help you with?'

'Harry. I'm here to help with anything you need. We only spoke a few days ago. I, I can't believe he's gone,' she said as tears began to well in her eyes.

'May I ask how you know about Mr. McKenzie's passing?'

She blinked rapidly and then smiled. 'I'll keep my sources private,' she said.

'Be that as it may, we listened to your podcast last night, and I think it was in poor taste. We haven't even had time to notify his family.'

'He has no family, detective. I am the closest thing he had to family.'

Nick was surprised at her comment. They must have been closer than he first thought. Perhaps even romantically linked, he wondered? 'Why don't you come through into our offices and have a chat? Would you like a cup of tea?' he asked.

He watched her shoulders drop slightly, the defensive tension in her body slowly leaving it, as she looked like she was in full preparation for a verbal stoush. 'I'd love one,' she said.

After the formal introductions were made, Nick, Maz, and Prue sat in the small interview room together. He had placed some of the Belle Smith investigation folders on the white table in between them and opened his notebook up to a fresh page.

She placed her hands on top of them with her eyes closed and spoke first. 'You know I have copies of every one of those. I feel like I know them from memory. I submitted Freedom of Information requests.'

Nick disagreed with certain aspects of the Freedom of Information Act, especially on cold, unsolved cases. He didn't believe access to sensitive information should be given out so freely to the public. 'I'm sure you do. Your work on the Smith disappearance is very impressive, and I'd like to discuss some aspects of that later. But first, Harry McKenzie, how long had you known him?'

'Around two years, I came across this case by chance. I grew up abroad as a kid, we lived in Japan. And I hadn't heard about her disappearance until I moved here when I was in Uni. I don't know what it was, but it always fascinated me, and I knew as soon as Dead Still got as popular as it did that I had to do this case. Harry emailed me last January. He read an article that mentioned the next case I was covering, and it started from there.'

'What was the nature of your relationship?' Maz asked.

'Platonic, I would say we really were more like friends than work colleagues. He was always so busy with work.' Her eyes began to well up again. 'I can't believe he is gone. Why would someone want to kill him?

'We don't have that answer yet, unfortunately,' Nick said.

'I know you're just going to say it's an ongoing investigation, but can you give me something? Anything? Can you tell me what happened?'

He knew the question was coming and was going back and forth in his mind about what decision he was about to make. Knowing the wealth of information she had in Belle's disappearance, he knew she could be a valuable asset, as long as she could keep it to herself for the time being.

'I can tell you that information, Miss Thornton. But first, I need some assurances from you.'

She wiped tears from her eyes and sat up expectantly.
'Like what?'

'I'm going to allow you to assist in this investigation if
you like. I have the authority to sign you on as a special
liaison officer. But I need your word that for now on there'll
be no more episodes, no more posts, nothing out of you until
we get to the bottom of all of this.'

He could see she was thinking it over. It was a good offer;
he knew it and she did, too. She smiled at the two officers,
and reached over the table, shaking their hands one by one.
'Done.'

Chapter Nineteen

Tom's house sat against the far back fence line of Belgrove, deep in the tree line, hidden out of sight. The end of the orange orchard sat only fifty metres from his front porch, and during seeding, the smell of pesticides filled his trailer for months on end. His brother and wife had offered a bedroom up at the house, but he enjoyed the privacy back here.

More an oversized caravan than demountable home, it sat up on thick stacks of concrete blocks and had a small makeshift deck. Lined with old and weathered pine boards, it formed a front veranda that spanned the length of the building.

Tom sat on the veranda on a faded green plastic chair and took a long swig out of a cold beer bottle. He hadn't anticipated the cop's visit to the farm yesterday, and if he'd known he would've moved all his product off site.

Once he moved back to Darfield, the years of work on the farm for his brother just weren't cutting it. His old contacts from the city had kept in touch, and he knew he was only a phone call away if he ever wanted to get involved in the business again and make some real money.

He started out small. Dealers would drop out product to him, which he kept in the small shed he built behind his trailer for storage. The police had begun to realise that the smaller country towns were becoming hot spots for party drugs in the 90s and early 2000s, and the bigger regional centres like Mildura were having multiple, big-time busts. His contacts were in front of them, though, and began to use Tom's farm as a storage centre for bigger, interstate movements. Arthur had hated the idea at first, but when money got tight, he reluctantly accepted and told Tom that no matter what, he had to keep it from Vanessa and the kids. The money was cut 50/50 between the brothers and had kept the farm afloat during the rougher years in the drought.

The detective yesterday on the farm had rattled him, and he hoped blabbing about Harry McKenzie might keep the heat off him for now. He felt a deep, lifelong guilt about his niece, and he had read about the Sydney detective in the paper last year. He had solved a couple of murders over in Milford. He knew he was going to be a tough customer.

It was all so long ago now; he remembered the lead up to the event and the fires like it was yesterday; it felt seared into his mind forever. He had made a stupid decision back then and ebbed and flowed between regret and disgust at his actions. But he ultimately knew she was gone now, and nothing was going to bring her back.

His phone buzzed loudly and broke him out of his daydream. He looked down at the small screen and cursed himself. Now was not the time.

'Tom, you right mate?' Came a voice from down the line. 'What's this I hear about some fella being murdered up your way? Is this going to become a problem for us?'

He knew the increased police presence was going to add an element of risk to the operation, but with the way this year's crops were looking, he couldn't afford to say no to the latest opportunity. Crystal meth, or ice as the dealers called it, had become a juggernaut in the bush and was the main drug stored on the farm these days.

'Next-door neighbour was found dead yesterday morning. Nothing we can't handle.'

'You got anything to do with it?'

He laughed. 'Nah. I knew the bloke, though. Shot Roo's over on the property for him only a few months ago, wasn't a bad kid.'

'So what happened to him?'

'Shot. He was a Private eye. I'm guessing someone got stiffed for something and finally had enough, found where he lived.'

'Cops been out your way yet?'

'Yep, yesterday. Had a quick chat to us about it and left.'

He listened to the voice breathing down the phone, the last big drop that had been stored on the farm had netted him ten thousand cash, the most he had ever made, he knew it was chump change to an operation the size of theirs, and he couldn't afford to lose this next drop. He was saving all the money to get away from Belgrove, once and for all.

'Right. It's all over the news today. I think we may need to hold off on our next shipment.'

'Nah, it should be f..'

The sharp click on the other end of the line let him know the call had ended.

Shit, he wanted that money badly. A few years earlier, when ice started to become the main drug being stored on the farm, Arthur had finally had enough and told his brother he wanted out of the operation. He strictly forbade him to continue it, and although he promised him, he was never going to let the opportunity slip, not when he was this close to having enough cash to leave the farm for good.

This detective was going to need to be sorted out. He just wasn't sure how yet. His sniffing around about Belle was not good, and he thought after all of this time, the heat would be off by now.

Her disappearance would come up now and again around the town, on anniversaries, and whenever he would see that stupid old missing poster. Art and Vanessa had gone on 60 minutes years earlier to try to drum up some interest, but nothing had ever come of it. Nothing seemed to have stuck until this podcast come out, whatever that is. But it was the talk of the town he knew, and whenever he went anywhere, people seemed to whisper in hushed tones. He didn't like it, but knew they were all barking up the wrong tree, anyway.

He sat and looked out at the stark, bare orange trees skirting the rear of the farm. Times were tougher than ever. There was no doubt about that. He had heard stories of farmers far and wide, finally giving up and taking their own lives. His phone rang and shook him from his dark thoughts. Seeing an unknown number, he answered straight away, hopeful his contact may have changed his mind.

'Hello?'

'Hello Tom, this is Detective Sergeant Nick Vada. We met yesterday.'

Shit, he didn't muck around this bloke. 'Yeah, I remember. What do you want? I've already told you everything I know.'

He really needed to clear out the last of his stash in case they did decide to visit.

'We are on our way out to you. Art said you were home, just a courtesy. We are five minutes away.'

He hung up and slammed his phone down on the old pallet table beside him. If Art knew what he still had stashed in the back shed, he wouldn't have sent them this way so quickly. He threw his empty beer in the old fuel drum off the side of his deck and quickly made his way around the back of the trailer to the small shed tucked in the back. He could see the dust cloud in the distance and knew they would be there shortly. Unlocking the padlock on the door, he quickly grabbed the containers of stock sitting on the bench top and swung up the checker plate steel trap door, revealing a small hollowed out storage bunker underneath the floor. As he placed the containers in gently and went to press the door down to close it, he noticed the old timber box sitting up on the cobwebbed covered top shelf. Not something they or anyone needs to see. He threw it too into the hole and pressed the trap door down with a click and dragged the rubber matt across the opening to hide it from view.

He raced back out the door and clicked the padlock shut. He'd worked up a sweat and quickly mopped his brow with his handkerchief that was sitting beside the shed entrance as he walked back around toward the front door of the trailer.

Standing at the foot of his deck, the detective and local sergeant eyed Tom with curiosity as he came walking round from the back of his home. 'You okay? You look like you've seen a ghost,' Nick said.

Tom wiped his brow again with his handkerchief in his left hand. He leaned at ease beside his trailer with a smile. That was a little too close for comfort, he thought to himself. 'Nah, just this sun. I don't exactly have the best AC out here,' he said, pointing towards the old trailer. 'As you can see, I don't live the life of luxury like the main house. The fire missed this place. I wasn't lucky enough to get a payout.'

'You think you were lucky?' Maz replied, 'A lot of people lost everything. I wouldn't call that lucky.'

'And you also lost your niece,' Nick added.

The three stood in an awkward silence. Nick didn't like the guy, and he knew he thought the same. There was something off about him that he just couldn't make out. He gave him a bad feeling, and those feelings were almost always right.

'So, what do ya's want?'

'Hoping to have a word if you have time?'

'Not really, but you've come all this way.' He walked up onto the small deck. Nick noted that there were four green plastic seats set up haphazardly on the deck, with multiple beer bottles, and ashtrays set around them. 'Take a seat,' he said, motioning to the chairs.

They set down together and Nick started. 'Looks like you have had a few visitors out here?'

Tom cursed himself silently. After the last drop off, some of the guys had stopped and had a beer before they left. He was meaning to clean it up before Arthur noticed anything. 'Just a couple of mates, nothing illegal in having a beer, is there?'

'Just making conversation,' he said, as he opened his notebook and sat it on his lap. He could sense that he was a little rattled. As he continued to sweat, he was constantly looking back toward the main farmhouse. 'So, we've spoken about Harry McKenzie. Arthur and Vanessa confirmed your whereabouts over the last few days. And we know what vehicle you own. I'm confident in thinking you weren't involved there.'

Nick wasn't confident at all at the time and wondered whether his previous life in the city had anything to do with the current events. Even though he didn't have a record, it didn't mean a thing to him. He may have just got smarter and better at hiding things. His main reason originally for coming to Darfield was to get justice for Belle Smith, and this murder gave him extra access to interview potential suspects for her disappearance, all while trying to catch Harry's killer. He was going to try to walk a delicate tightrope, but it was one he had walked before.

'Okay,' Tom replied, 'So, what are you here for then?'

'I'd like to discuss the days up to and after Belle's disappearance. It looks to me like you were never formally interviewed, which I'd like to change. You may hold the key in unlocking any information we need to help find out what happened to her.'

Tom got up and walked inside the trailer. Nick looked over at Maz with a questioning shrug. Soon he returned with a beer, and cracked the top off, flicking the empty lid into a drum beside the deck. He was prepared for these questions and knew sooner or later they'd be asked, and he had his answers carefully rehearsed.

'What do you want to know?'

Chapter Twenty

They went through the timeline of Belle's disappearance, And Nick heard all the same beats he had heard and read so far before. Deciding to change tact, he asked, 'So, how did she seem in the weeks leading up to her disappearance? I've heard that she seemed a lot quieter than usual?'

'Nah, not really. She was her same usual self. I saw nothing different there.'

Nick wrote in his notepad and tried to buy some time. Sometimes he would just scribble random notes, the act of writing on the pad causing distress for the interviewee.

'Actually,' Tom said, 'I guess she may have seemed a bit off, like I said the other day. Harry McKenzie was harassing the poor girl. She was probably terrified.'

He wondered just how bad this so-called harassment was to a couple of teenage girls, and whether it was just more of a teenage crush. A young boy not knowing the correct way to express his feelings, and maybe coming off as slightly unusual.

'And you spoke with Harry's father?'

'Yep, I bailed him up in the pub about it. Told him to stay away from my niece. Fat luck it did. He obviously had something to do with it, otherwise, why would he accuse Art of killing her?'

Now they were starting to get somewhere. 'Is that why he and Vanessa had a falling out?'

'Your damn right it is, he was up at the house for months on end, him and Vanessa pouring themselves over the old case files, maps, reports of sightings of her, testing of the pieces of the house for DNA, you name it. The bloke was leading her on, obviously, trying to divert the blame away from himself. And then he goes on this stupid fucking podcast and blames my brother for it! He's lucky I didn't get my hands on him after I found that out.'

'Well, Arthur did have a history,' he replied, poking him now to see his reaction.

'My brother isn't a killer detective, and neither am I, for that matter.'

'So, what do you think happened to Belle, then?' Maz asked.

Tom swigged from his beer bottle and sighed. 'McKenzie stalked her for months. She told me that. He's spent the best part of two years trying to pin my brother on the crime. He was only a kid then, but he was always a weird little bastard. I don't know what happened to Belle, but I could guarantee you he had something to do with it. And he's dead now, so fucked if I know how you're going to get any answers. Will that be all?'

He could tell that Tom wasn't going to say anything he hadn't heard already from someone else before. He stood up and Maz followed his lead.

'Thanks for your help, Tom,' Maz replied.

The two detectives stood up, and Nick looked out across the bare orchards. 'Hey Tom?' he asked.

The man now looked even more disgruntled, thinking they were about to leave, when he replied, 'What?'

'What happened to the Darfield orange? From all reports, business was booming out here back in the day?'

Tom sighed. 'Some lab in Europe figured out how to copy it, sweeter and even better than ours. And better growing conditions over there.' He held his arms out wide, signalling the predicament they were in. 'Which leaves us here how we are now, pretty much up shit creek.'

***

Driving back towards Darfield, Nick passed the second news van he'd seen for the day. White with Channel Four emblazoned across the side and back, it had a giant satellite dish folded down across the roof. Things were about to get crazy, he thought and asked Maz how she thought their chat had gone. 'What do you think?'

'About Tom? Honestly, we never looked too hard into him. He helped in the search back then and never caused us any concern. He and Art both have their records, but you can see they both seem to be fairly helpful.'

There was still something about the man that didn't feel right in Nick, and he decided to keep his suspicions to himself for now and try to keep his options open, but he knew his gut feelings were usually right.

'Fair enough. I think we need to arrange that press conference, looking at the amount of news trucks we've seen today. They are going to want an update on where we are at with the investigation. We need to stay in front of this.'

'But we don't have much?' she asked.

'A problem police have for a lot of these,' he said with a laugh. 'We might look like we know what we are doing in the city, sergeant, but sometimes we are flying blind just as much as we are right now. The best thing about these is sometimes we get tips. And that's what we need right now.'

They turned right into the entrance of the McKenzie farm and, sitting in the table drain, a black ABC news truck sat at an awkward angle. Standing beside the entrance to the gate, a cameraman filmed a blond woman in a teal green pantsuit and a rain jacket, with a boom microphone held directly above her head.

'Is that Jennifer Oswald?' Maz asked. 'She's shorter in person.'

'Looks like it.'

Once they parked, Maz walked off to check in with Samantha, who was onsite aiding the crime scene services team. Nick walked over to the small white gazebo towards Bec and watched her taking images of items strewn across the small tables. She was incredibly thorough and worked with rehearsed precision; she was much too good at her job to be doing this in the bush.

She stood up from her screen and smiled in his direction. 'I was just about to call you.'

'You were?'

'I was. We may have found something.'

Walking back towards the house, Nick yelled out to Maz and Samantha to follow. Bec walked up the back steps of the house and stopped at the rear entrance of the house.

'We've searched the house thoroughly, haven't found a huge amount. He was a bachelor and lived here alone. It was mostly extremely clean, almost to the point of obsessive-compulsive for a house that has sat for a few days. The only evidence we found of another living thing in this house was a bit of dog hair from his dog, Bailey.'

'Okay,' Nick replied. 'So why are we here?'

'Dust,' Bec replied.

'Dust? What about it?'

'There were footsteps throughout the house, but mostly through the main hallway. Now we've deduced when you and Sergeant Rogers have come through, and we know where Harry had been, but we found something unusual. Traces of bright red dirt have been traipsed down this hallway, the dirt here in the Mallee is completely different. We've taken a couple of samples and under a microscope we believe it's from nowhere near here. Looks more like dirt from the outback, I'm guessing far north Queensland.'

'Queensland? That is unusual.' He immediately thought of the sprawling, wide landscapes of outback Queensland. The bright red dust would go everywhere, all through the vents of your car, your clothes, and your body. The heat was relentless up there. A few hours outside during the summer months would prove fatal for anyone not prepared. Countless backpackers had gone missing throughout the years up there, and it was an inhospitable place.

'We'll do further testing. It might be nothing.'

'No, it's good work. It could mean a lot of things,' he said, still thinking about Tom Smith and the drugs in his past life. 'Let's keep our options open.'

He walked back to his car after their discussion and headed back into town alone. Hearing his phone ring, he was surprised to see a FaceTime call incoming. His sister Jess was the only one to ever FaceTime him, and he felt awkward sometimes seeing his face reflected back at him. He indicated off the main road, and pulled off to the side, muting his car radio and pressing the answer button.

The screen made a small beep, and Jess stared back at him with a glowing smile on her face. She had had a rough year the year previous, with Nick accusing her husband of being a murderer and all. With all of that in the past, the couple had been busy on their sprawling property, Warranilla, and were expecting their first child in the months to come. The thought of having a nephew was still foreign to him, but he liked the fact that it gave him an excuse to head home more often than usual. Although he had promised to be around more, work had kept him away for the past six months.

'Big brother. You're a hard person to get onto,' she said.

'Sorry, sis, you know how it is. Work. How are you feeling?'

She stood up to show off her now watermelon size bump and rubbed it proudly with her hands. 'It's like a little basketball attached to my front now, getting harder and harder to get stuff done around the house, but Pete's been good to me, I'm trying to put my feet up and he's been helping out as much as he can.'

Nick saw another face pop in from the side of the screen, her husband, Pete Waterford. He was the heir to one of the biggest properties around his hometown, and although under the circumstances he came into it, had worked hard, and had pulled the farm away from financial ruin, ensuring his sister and nephew a long and prosperous future.

'Nick, you well mate?'

'Great, thanks Pete. Hope you're looking after her.'

'Always mate, she's a stubborn one, though. I can't get her to sit still! Anyway, I've got to head out to service the headers. I'll see you, mate.'

He was a hard worker; he couldn't fault him there. 'Never switches off.' Jess sighed.

'How's the pregnancy going?' He realised after asking her that he had only spoken to her once since she told him she was due. He felt guilty for not keeping up with her more.

'Yeah, it's been okay. I've through the morning sickness now, spent a month sitting on the bathroom floor, but I'm past that now.'

'Jesus, that sounds terrible, sis. You seen Jack and Nell?'

Jack and Nell Thomson had been like a second mother and father to himself and Jess during their childhood, and Nick was as close to the two as his sister.

'Yeah, Nell was out yesterday. She has been whipping up some meals for me for when the bub comes. She's also given me plenty of dates.'

'Dates?' he asked, confused.

She chuckled. 'They're meant to bring on labour, apparently. I've googled it but can't tell if it's actually a thing, or an old wives' tale, but hey, I'll try anything when it gets to go time.'

They sat in silence for a short second, and she asked. 'So, where are you right now? I tried your home phone and got no answer, although who knows why I try, you never answer it.'

Nick knew as soon as he said where he was that his sister would worry. 'I'm in Darfield, kinda' near you.'

'Darfield? That was on the news just before, some farmer was killed yesterday. Gee, they got you up there quick?'

'Yeah, I guess, I didn't have as much on my plate as some others. Mark was trying to give me some time off. I must have pulled the short straw.'

'Darfields where that young girl went missing years ago, wasn't it? I remember seeing it all over the news, Belle, something?'

'Smith.'

'That's it. This got anything to do with it?'

'That's what I'm here to find out.'

She laughed. 'Of course you are. Well, if anyone's going to do it, it'll be you.'

'Thanks Sis, hey listen, I've got a press conference to attend so I better get going.'

'Right. I'll keep the TV on.'

He chuckled at that. 'Thanks, I'll talk to you soon.'

Chapter Twenty-One

Belle and Anna sat in Anna's bedroom. They listened to the cassette tape they had recorded a few nights ago and danced along to their favourite songs.

'So, did you get it?' Anna asked.

Belle smiled at her friend and grabbed her handbag from Anna's bedside table. She reached into the small, sequined bag and pulled out her purse. Opening it up and flicking through her cards, she pulled out a driver's licence and handed it over to Anna.

Anna held up the fake ID, which was a NSW driver's licence, with Belle's photo expertly printed on it. The name on it read, 'Britney Rearden.' Her address was listed as 77 Oaks Court, Darfield.

'Britney Rearden?'

'Yeah, well Britney's all the rage now, isn't she? And Rearden, I just made up.'

'You think it'll work?'

'Yeah, as long as we don't see Maz Rogers in there, or any of Mum or Dad's friends. He said yours will be ready next week.'

The girls had been told for the entirety of last year about one of the boys in their classes cousin who had a contact at the motor registry. This contact could expertly print out 'replacement' driver's licences at $100 each. All the buyer had to do was supply a licence photo and give them whatever information they required. The girls didn't believe them at the start, but when the boys started flashing the replica licences, they were intrigued. There was nothing to do in Darfield, and a chance to drink at the only pub legally in town a year early was too good to miss.

'Cool,' Anna said. She was secretly a bit worried about the whole endeavour, and although Belle looked grown up, she still felt like she looked fourteen. She imagined walking into the pub and being walked straight out the door again, humiliated in front of Belle and all her friends.

'Yeah, I can't wait.'

Anna's Mum popped her head into the door, and Belle scrambled quickly, throwing the replica licence under Anna's pillow.

'You girls need anything before bed?' she asked.

'No Mum, we're fine. We're just putting on a movie.'

'Okay, goodnight.'

The girls sat quietly and watched the scary movie on Anna's small tv on her dresser. They sat close together, and Belle could feel Anna jump at some of the scarier scenes. As they began to get towards the end, she thought she saw the flash of a light coming from Anna's window, and got up to investigate. 'What was that?' she asked Anna.

'What?'

'I swear I saw a light out there?'

'I didn't see anything? You know that back lane. It's a dead end. No one ever comes down here.'

The girls sat back down and turned the movie on. Minutes later, they heard a bang and a clatter right underneath the window. Anna screamed, and it woke up the house, with her father running in and opening the door wide. 'You girls all good in here?'

'Someone's at the window, Dad!'

Anna's Dad ran back down the hallway. Belle looked at Anna and the girls took off, following. Getting into the laneway, Anna's Dad yelled out, 'Oi! Come here!' at the skinny figure sprinting down the back lane away from them. He turned and looked back at the girls. 'Any ideas who that was?'

'None,' Anna said, who was now terrified after watching the scary movie.

When the girls got back into the bedroom, Anna switched the TV off. Belle sat on the edge of the bed and looked rattled. Anna realised she hadn't said anything since the encounter and looked scared. 'You ok?' she asked.

'Yeah, I'm okay. You said you didn't know what that was?'

'Yeah, no idea?'

'It was Harry McKenzie, I'm sure of it.'

Anna thought of Harry McKenzie and the figure running through the night. It certainly could've been him, she thought, but what was the obsession with Belle? 'No way, surely not?'

'I swear it was. I'm starting to really get freaked out An, this is the third time.'

Anna knew her friend and knew that she was a tough customer, and that this was starting to get to her. What she thought was just an innocent crush felt more serious now.

'This is getting crazy. Should we talk to someone?' she asked.

'I already have. I spoke to my uncle about it. He said he was going to sort it out.'

She thought of Tom and him sitting on the bed the week previous. Her mind trailed off, and she began to daydream.

'You ok?' Belle asked.

She snapped back to reality. 'Yeah, sorry.'

The next day, the girls sat in front of the local café waiting for their friend to arrive. Belle lounged back on the wicker chair, with her long legs stretched out onto the café table, glistening in the afternoon sunlight. If she was still worried about Harry McKenzie, she didn't show it, Anna thought, and wondered how the girls were going to tackle their problem.

A white ute came roaring around the corner into the main street, with dark tinted windows and P plates. The music in the car was loud enough that the girls could hear every lyric. Pulling into the café storefront, Billy Thommers got out and waved at the two girls to come over.

Anna watched Belle get up from the café chair and put on her best smile. Billy was in the same year as the girls and had been using his fake ID to get into the local pub for the last few months with no dramas. She still didn't like the idea, but knew if she didn't go, then Belle wouldn't either, and she felt the peer pressure weighing on her.

'Belle, how are ya?' Billy asked, completely ignoring Anna.

Anna watched the young man, leaning against his driver's side door. He was tall and had a blond undercut with stubble just beginning to grow from his chin. He was wearing red football shorts and a black singlet, and his muscular arms stood out. He was turning into a man before their eyes, and Anna could tell Belle also liked what she saw.

'Good thanks Billy, you got what I asked for?'

He reached into his glove compartment and pulled out a giant folder of CD's. Unzipping the front pocket, he pulled the driver's licence out and held it up to them. 'There ya go, one of his best, I reckon. Looks dead on.' He looked over in Anna's direction. 'Hey An.'

Anna blushed. 'Hi Billy.'

'Don't fuck this up for us,' he said, handing her the card. 'If anyone catches you, just make something up. If my cousin gets caught for this, he's going to jail.'

That comment made her even more nervous. She was only eight months away from being eighteen. What was the rush?

Belle smirked at Anna. 'Don't be ridiculous, Billy, no one's going to jail, we're big girls, we can handle ourselves.'

'Fair enough. Hey, what are you up to this arvo? Want to go for a cruise?'

Belle looked at Billy and smiled. 'Thanks for the offer, but we've got to get ready for the pub tonight.'

'Your loss,' he said, and with that, he jumped back into the ute and roared off in the direction he came.

'You ready for your first night on the town?' Belle asked.

Chapter Twenty-Two

Later that night, the girls got ready together in Anna's bedroom. She watched as Belle completed the last of her makeup and finished it off with pale pink lipstick. She wore a denim skirt with a light blue top and had her long hair tied up in a messy bun. She spun around in a tight circle when she was finished, looking at Anna for approval. 'What do you think? Do I look old enough?'

'You look great,' Anna replied. She had decided on something a bit more muted, dark black jeans and a cream-coloured singlet top. She thought that she needed to dress older, considering she looked much younger than her age suggested.

Sensing Anna's lack of enthusiasm, Belle asked, 'You okay?'

'Yeah, I'm alright, I just don't want to get busted.'

Belle wrapped her arm around her shoulder. 'Don't worry about that An, we're girls. Everyone will look the other way. Billy said Tarissa and Chloe last year got in with no dramas. We'll be fine.'

'If you say so.'

As the girls walked out the front door of the shop, Anna's Mum came out of the dining room to wave them off goodbye. 'Far out. You girls look great. Where are you off to?'

'Just a party Mum, we won't be home late.'

'Fair enough, be safe please, and if you need a lift, give me a call.'

They made the short walk to the pub quickly, and as they got near the front entrance, a car flew past and tooted its horn, with a drunk person hanging out the window yelling, 'Looking good ladies!'

Belle rolled her eyes. 'Well, at least we have one admirer.'

As they got to the front door, a small line had formed down one side. They could hear loud music, and multi-coloured lights flashed from inside the windows. 'There's a DJ tonight. Can't wait to have a dance,' Belle said.

Anna was now terrified at the thought of being knocked back by the tall security guard standing at the entrance of the door, as they got to the front of the line she fumbled for her ID in her purse, and managed to pull it out just as they got to him.

The bouncer looked them up and down. 'Evening ladies, you from around here?'

'Just here for the night,' Belle replied with her best smile.

'Have fun,' he said, waving them both on through.

Anna walked over the threshold into the heaving pub. Towards the back of the room where the bistro usually was, had been cleared out, and a DJ was setup in the far back corner with an elaborate light display flashing and reflecting colourful lights on and through into the front bar. Over on the main bar, it was two deep with patrons, all jostling to get a drink. Dan Rogers, the publican, was pouring bright green liquid into a row of shot glasses for a group of girls standing in the centre. She couldn't believe how easy it was to get in and felt a rush of excitement at being in this forbidden place.

'Well, that was a lot easier than I thought,' she said to Belle over the music.

'Let's get a drink!' she replied.

The two girls ran into some of their school friends, and most of them Anna realised now, had fake IDs as well. She had been drinking since she was fourteen, sneaking the odd drink away from her Mum and Dad's stash, and getting six packs from Belle's uncle. She had developed a pretty good tolerance for it compared to some of her school friends, including Belle, who by now were absolutely wasted.

As the night wore on, some of their friends began to leave, and she realised that it was starting to get late, and her Mum would be wondering where she was. She watched as Belle sat beside an older man, deep in conversation. With a bright green button up work shirt and mesh trucker cap, he looked to be in his early twenties. Smiling and laughing like it was any other weekend, she looked at ease talking with him, and Anna sensed a lot of flirting going on.

She yelled over the music in their direction. 'Hey Belle, Loo?'

Belle looked over in her direction with bleary eyes and a drink in her hand. 'I'm good An.'

She felt a bit left out and was starting to get frustrated with Belle. They planned to see if the IDs worked, have a few drinks, and get out before Anna's Mum worried. She could tell now that her friend was getting drunk and was worried she might be getting herself into trouble. Looking at her watch, it was now 11:15, and way past when she told her Mum she'd be home.

Once she'd gone to the toilet, she washed her hands quickly and looked in the mirror. I just need to be strong. Walk over there and tell her we are going, she thought. Steeling herself for a potentially awkward conversation, she pushed open the bathroom door and ran almost headfirst into Maz Rogers, who was in full police uniform. Feeling her blood go cold, she tried to keep her head down, hoping she wouldn't recognise her.

'Anna?' Maz said to her back as she walked away.

Feeling the air go out of her lungs, she turned, ready to face the music. 'Hi Maz. How are you?'

'I'm fine, thank you. Now I know what year you're in at school, love, and I don't think you're eighteen yet, are you?'

'No, I'm not,' she replied, defeated.

'I'm not going to make a big deal out of this. All you kids try it, I just expected better from you. I'm happy to keep your Mum and Dad out of it, but please don't try to come in here again, yeah?'

'I won't.'

She looked over toward the main bar. 'Now, who else are you here with?'

Anna looked over towards the table that they had all been sitting at and found it empty. 'Just me,' she replied.

Maz looked at her, and she could tell she didn't believe her. She sighed. After a long day, this was the least of her problems dealing with underage kids in her pub. 'Fair enough, you get home safe, please.'

Anna walked out of the pub and back towards home, furious that Belle had left her alone. As she walked, she began to cry, feeling the tears streaking down her face. Just as she turned off the main street, she noticed two people walking ahead of her, and could tell straight away that the girl on the left was Belle. Barely being able to walk straight, the man in the green shirt half-walked and half-stumbled, trying to hold her up. Anna began to run, soon catching up with the two after a block. 'Hey Belle! You ditched me back there!' she yelled.

The man in the green shirt turned around and looked at Anna in disgust. She could tell now when Belle faced her that she was completely out of it, her eyes only half open and her legs barely holding her weight.

'Oh, it's you. What do you want?' he asked.

She had had enough by then and wasn't prepared to be told what to do by this man, who was clearly trying to take advantage of her best friend. She burst out. 'What do I want? I want my friend, you creep! Can't you see she's wasted? Fuck off or I'll call the cops!'

The man blinked twice, and removed his arm from underneath Belle's shoulder, pushing her towards Anna. She stepped quickly, and she had to catch her before she fell headfirst onto the pavement. 'She's all yours,' he said with a grunt, as he disappeared into the darkness.

Chapter Twenty-Three

Nick sat back inside the police station, flanked by Maz, Prue, and Pat. He was looking up at the TV mounted on the wall and watched himself talking on the national news. He hated watching himself on TV and felt that his delivery felt forced and formal, wishing he had the laid back, authoritative style that some of his colleagues had when running them.

A large swathe of reporters stood in front of the Darfield police station, in the small fenced off front yard. Maz told him she hadn't seen that many cars in the street since the weeks after Belle disappeared, and it was a stark reminder of what he was here for.

The reporters had done most of the talking, asking all the questions he knew they'd ask. Interestingly, Prue Thornton had remained quiet at the back of the scrum, watching intently with her recorder out. As he felt like they were running out of questions about Harry McKenzie, Jennifer Oswald, the reporter they'd seen earlier, asked the question he knew they all had wanted to ask. 'Mr. McKenzie was an acquaintance of Belle Smith, was he not? Does his death have anything to do with her disappearance?'

He knew his answer was going to set off a bombshell, and hoped that with the raised media scrutiny, further information might come out of the woodwork. 'Yes, Mr. McKenzie knew Belle Smith, and yes, we have reason to believe his murder may be linked to her disappearance.'

In that instance, multiple flashes of cameras seem to go off at once, and he felt the collective scrum of media pull in tighter, with multiple reporters yelling over the top of each other to get the next question in.

'What did you find detective!?' 'Did he kill Belle Smith!?' 'Have you found her body detective?!'

Maz switched the TV off in the station and looked back at Nick. 'Well, that went about as well as I thought it could. You're a braver man than me, detective.'

'Sadly, it's a part of my job. I hate doing them, but we need all the help we can get right now. Pat, have you or Sam had any luck with the gun register?'

Pat raced back over to his desk and logged into his computer. Reading from the screen, he wanted to give Nick the correct information. '795 guns that shoot 308 casings were sold in this region over the last ten years, and 458 of them had scopes. Now we know that the killer may have bought the scope separately, so we are still searching through both avenues, although until we find any bullets, we don't have much to go on.'

'Good work. Maz, any luck with the APB?'

'Sam put it in straight away. We've had a few tips, but as you know, a white Toyota Landcruiser ute is about the most popular car there is in this region. Hard to tell what a false sighting is, and what is legit.'

He thought of Harry's last few moments again, the sighting of the ute and the hole in his chest. 'Any news back from the autopsy?'

'Yes, we got it back this morning.' She threw another copy of the report over to him and they both read the copies at the same time. He knew that Harry's career as a private investigator was a tricky profession, and some of them were brilliant operators, able to get to the bottom of things without the bureaucracy of the law. They skirted in the grey areas and often had no moral boundaries. He had heard stories earlier in his career of private eyes in the old days getting involved in organised crime, with some never to be seen again.

He looked over to Maz. 'Do we know exactly what cases he was working on?'

She was halfway through lighting another cigarette and shrugged. 'No idea. I know he works for a couple of companies from Mildura, and I heard his main employer was QBE Insurance.'

'Insurance?' Pat asked, 'What insurance company needs a private investigator?'

Nick answered his question. 'It goes like this. Man hurts back at work supposedly, sues company, and lives off a healthy work cover monthly payment for the rest of his life. It's a private eyes job to watch them go about their day-to-day business, and hopefully catch them in the act doing things that would negate that claim. Person washing their car for example. How could they do that with a back injury?'

'I never thought of it like that,' Pat said. 'He would've been busy.'

'Yep, and an easy way to make enemies,' he said.

Prue had sat quietly off to the side of the group, and he noticed her watching intently. He knew she was smart and wanted to know her opinion on the investigation so far. 'What do you think, Prue?'

Opening her notepad, she cleared her throat awkwardly and began, 'Harry, dead by gunshot. Dust throughout the house from Queensland, a white work ute seen in the vicinity, and Belle's school dress found in his shed. A lot of contradictions here. I think it all still boils down to Belle, though, as much as I know you don't want to hear it.'

'How so?' Maz asked.

'The dress. How and why did it get to Harry's farm? And when? That's the biggest clue here. I think it's pretty clear how it got there.'

'Go on,' he said.

'The Smiths. I think Arthur planted it and he killed Harry. Harry had accused him to one of the biggest audiences this case had ever seen. My podcast had ten million listeners per episode, the biggest in Australia. I had tips coming in from all over, and who knows what it brought up here in Darfield? I think when Vanessa told him that Harry had accused him of killing her, he sat on it for the last few weeks boiling with anger, and even Vanessa trying to clear his name on the last episode wasn't enough. I think he finally snapped, drove to the farm, and shot Harry dead.'

'It's an interesting theory, but why did he wait so long?'

'It's hard to know. Maybe he didn't even know Harry had accused him until the last few days? Maybe Vanessa kept it from him. She told me he never listened to the podcast. Could you imagine? After years and years of gossip and innuendo around the town, maybe hearing what Harry said, something broke inside of him. We all have seen his temper.'

'What about the brother, Tom Smith?' he asked.

'Harry and I both looked into his back story. There isn't much to know. He's not Arthur's brother, you know, he's his stepbrother. He was adopted.'

'I didn't know that,' Maz said.

'It's not really common knowledge,' she said. 'He has stayed loyal to Arthur, though. He has lived on Belgrove for years. He was a bit wilder when he was younger from what we found out, but never caused much fuss.'

'He used to spend a fair bit of time in the pub. Dan used to say he could drink most of them in there under the table. Something changed after the fires, though. We didn't see him as much as we used to. Anna Denholm might be a good one to ask. She used to spend time with him and Belle when they were kids.'

'I think I might pay her a visit,' he said. He looked at the team and decided it might be best if he go at it alone. He felt like Anna might open up to him more if he didn't have any locals around.

Chapter Twenty-Four

Nick made the drive to the outskirts of town back out towards the general store. He passed a very new-looking BP fuel service station and wondered just how long the small store would be able to survive with their new competition.

He tried to map out all the pieces in front of him as he drove and struggled to find a connecting thread to put it all together. Why was Harry McKenzie murdered? And if Arthur Smith had something to do with it, why now? He had been accused before of the same crime, in newspapers and even on national TV, and had still managed to mostly keep his cool. Was it a matter of the final straw? Years and years of finger pointing he snapped, and couldn't take it anymore? Or was it something simpler, a bad private eye job gone wrong, a client unhappily wronged by Harry and deciding to get revenge?

He pulled into the dirt carpark in front of the building and noticed a white ute fuelling up at the single pump. There was just no way that APB was going to find anything. The amount of white work utes in this country would be in the tens of thousands. He made a mental note to tell Maz to drop it. Unless they had a registration, they were grasping at straws.

He walked past the old farmer, who leaned against the ute tray with a slight nod and a smile. He had a long grey beard and was scratching an old blue heeler under the chin that sat obediently on the back of the tray. At least some locals looked to be remaining loyal.

Walking past the missing poster for Belle again he made his way through the old store and up to the counter, and was surprised to see a teenage girl sitting there, with fair blond hair and a pale complexion she had brilliant blue eyes and was deep into something on her iPhone screen. He cleared his throat loudly when he realised she hadn't noticed him standing in front of her. 'Uh-erm.'

She jumped and looked up from her screen. 'Oh my god, I'm sorry! Just the fuel?'

As soon as she spoke, he realised that she must be Anna's daughter. He could see the resemblance straight away. He didn't realise she had kids. 'Ahh, no, I was wondering if Anna was around?'

The girl looked Nick up and down and smiled. 'Muuum!' she yelled towards the back of the store. 'You must be Nick, the hot detective.'

He felt his face go red with embarrassment as Anna came round the corner, hearing the end of their conversation. 'Brooke Denholm! Out the back now, please!' she said, with her complexion matching Nick's. Brooke giggled and rushed down the long counter and out through the back doorway.

'Sorry about that,' Anna said. 'Kids.'

'No problems at all,' he replied awkwardly. 'Hoping you had a minute to chat?'

She smiled. 'I wondered when you would turn up. Surprised it took so long.'

They sat out at the back of the old general store in a makeshift outdoor dining area. A huge acacia tree sat in the centre of the yard, providing ample shade for them as they sat at a well-worn picnic table with bench seats.

'Covid outdoor dining,' she said to Nick as he looked around the small area. 'Had to adapt to survive.'

'Looking at that BP on the way into town, it looks like the battle is still in front of you.'

'Yep, that one caught me off guard. The old Ampol at the other end of town has been more than capable for the past 30 years. I wasn't sure how BP thought it was going to be profitable. But if it causes us to close and the Ampol to close, well, they'll have the monopoly in town, won't they?'

'I guess so. Although looking out the front just before, looks like you've still got some loyal customers?'

'Loyalty only gets you so far, Nick. When they start getting fuel and food for 30% cheaper up there, we'll soon see who is loyal.'

It was the way things were going in all small communities. Bigger companies would come in, and with buying power could keep the prices low, pushing out all the local family-run businesses. Supermarkets were usually the first to go, and then it would continue from there. Most business owners who were forced to sell ended up working back at their old businesses for half the wage.

'Well, I know you're not here to talk about my business. I saw the news. What do you want to know?'

Nick opened his notepad up on the bench. 'You were interviewed once. Twenty-two years ago. I read that transcript. Two detectives from Sydney interviewed you. You were eighteen years old, probably scared to death for your friend and not knowing what to say and what not to say, not wanting to get yourself or her into any more trouble. Your best friends' parents were being accused of murder. I can understand the predicament you must have felt yourself in.'

Anna looked out towards the trunk of the Acacia tree with a sad expression. 'It was just all crazy back then. The fires were the worst this town has ever seen. I would say at least half of our family and friends at the time lost their homes or businesses. It felt like the town had nearly lost everything, and Belle disappearing was the cherry on top of it all.'

Nick nodded along in agreement. 'I know you were asked back then, but it's been so long. What do you think happened to her?'

She looked back from the tree directly into his eyes and asked, 'Can you tell me what you found at Harry McKenzie's?'

'I can't divulge information about an active investigation. I'm sorry, but as I said in the press conference, we found evidence tying him to Belle's disappearance.'

She began to sob quietly, and he sat silently, letting her compose herself before she continued. She spoke clearly and laid out her experience with Harry McKenzie from their youth, from him stalking Belle at her work all the way up to the night Belle thought she saw him at her window. Nick scribbled some notes in his notepad as she spoke, and he began to see a better timeline of what Tom Smith had told him earlier that week.

'So you think Harry McKenzie had something to do with it?' he asked when she finished.

'Has to be. I don't think you understand, Nick. She was really scared of him.'

'And why didn't you say anything to the detectives back then when they interviewed you?'

She shrugged. 'Honestly? I wasn't sure whether I believed Belle back then. And he has been nothing but a gentleman since her disappearance. He would pop out from time to time to the shop and was always generous. He came and asked me questions from time to time about Belle. I know he was helping Ness with her disappearance. But now he's dead, and you're saying you've found something on his farm. I guess all I think is that he was doing his best to divert attention away from himself.'

It was the second time he had heard the theory, and it seemed like a stretch to him. Why go to so much work to solve Belle's disappearance if he himself had something to do with it? He needed to look closer into Harry's past and try to get to the bottom of what he had to do with Belle's disappearance. Maybe they were connected, and by solving one, he solved the other.

She continued, 'I don't think Arthur and Vanessa have anything to do with it, as far as I'm concerned. Vanessa has never stopped from the moment Belle disappeared. She led the search on the farm, she constantly harassed the police and the papers to keep running stories about it, she worked with Prue on that podcast, she's been relentless.'

'And how about you? Did you help search the farm?'

She wiped the tears from her eyes and sighed. 'I did at first. And I saw the house. And the farm after the fires. Everything was destroyed. Back then, I kind of agreed with the police. I thought she had died in that house. I've thought about that for the longest time. But now all of this is coming out about Harry, my mind isn't totally made up. It was a long time ago, Nick. My life has moved on. I moved away, got married, had Brooke, got divorced and now I'm back to where I started. Sometimes I dream that she's out there somewhere, living a happy life. Wouldn't that be nice?'

It was wishful thinking he thought to himself. 'It would be, but from all reports, she was a happy kid, looking forward to life after school. Why would she run away?'

'I know, it's wishful thinking,' Anna replied sadly.

'So, Tom Smith, what do you know about him?'

'He was always around when me and Belle were younger. They were super close. He'd take us away camping when we were little girls. I even had a bit of a crush myself when I was a teenager. But when Belle disappeared, he changed. He was a different person. I've only spoken to him a handful of times since back then. He shut off. People grieve differently, I guess.'

Nick wasn't sure whether it was really grief, or something else entirely. 'Do you think he could have had anything to do with Belle's disappearance?'

'I don't know. Back then I would have said 100% not. He was at the front of the search on the farm back then. He and Arthur searched Belgrove and the surrounding farms day and night. The fires had destroyed most of those properties, of course, but that didn't stop them. Now, as the years have gone on, who knows? Like I said, he seems a different person after the fires. There could be plenty of reasons for that. He took us camping only two weeks before the fires. We went down to Lake Somerstead.'

He tried to imagine the days after the fires, the uncertainty, the confusion, and the loss. It would have been hard on everyone, especially those that lost their homes and belongings. He had Harry, who had Belle's school dress on his property, murdered in cold blood. And Tom Smith, although no evidence pointed in his direction, he couldn't shake the feeling something wasn't right with him, and he could feel Anna holding back as they spoke, like she was leaving words unsaid.

He closed his notebook, ending their formal interview. 'I think that's all I need for now, but if you can think of anything else, just let me know.'

'There is one more thing, and I don't know if it ever came up during the investigation.'

'Yeah?'

Anna picked at the edge of the picnic table, and he could tell she was uncomfortable. 'Belle had a fake ID. I had one too. We bought them from a school friend a couple of months before the fires. We used them to get into the pub.'

He hadn't heard anything of a fake ID. That opened some new avenues of investigation for him. He knew back in the late 90s early 2000s that the fake identification business was a prolific one. He himself had friends in his school that had picture perfect driver's licences. He was lucky that he looked old enough to walk into any pub back then, and he had taken advantage of it.

'That's interesting, and I'm guessing you never told the detectives because you were underage? And didn't want to get into trouble?'

'Bingo.'

He continued scribbling notes as he asked, 'Do you know if she went by her same name on the ID or any other name?'

'Another name. Britney Reardon.'

Chapter Twenty-Five

Tom Smith sat in his old work ute and let it idle, with his stepbrother by his side. They had a busy day ahead with seeding, and he knew he was going to have to face Arthur sooner or later.

'What did that detective want with you?' Arthur asked.

'He wanted to know about Belle. He asked if I had anything to do with her disappearance.'

'Jesus Christ, have they got no shame? What a load of bullshit. These coppers just don't quit, do they? Why the hell do they think you're involved?'

'Beats me. That copper has a bee in his bonnet. I don't think he likes me for some reason or another.'

Arthur looked through the front windscreen of the ute and tried to make sense of the last few days. Harry McKenzie, dead next door. And now the police were back on their doorstep, bringing up Belle again. He hadn't had much to do with Harry growing up and after his parents died, he barely saw the man, but he knew Tom had spoken with him only a couple of weeks ago and did the odd cash jobs on his property for him.

He glimpsed Tom's right forearm, and could see small scabs across his sun-tanned arm, a sure sign that he was using again. He was fiercely loyal to his little brother, but he had had to cover for him for his whole life, and when he brought drugs onto the farm, it was the final straw for him. The money had been good and had helped them survive when times were tough, but when he discovered that Tom was using again he had put a stop to the whole enterprise, he'd lost his daughter and he wasn't about to lose his brother too.

'Do you have any idea what happened to Harry?' he asked.

'No idea.'

'Weren't you out shooting there the other week?'

Tom scratched at the scab on his arm. 'Yeah, couple of Roo's out back had damaged his back fence, got two of them and fixed the fence up.'

'Did you hear the shots I heard the other day? I swore I heard shots. I saw a cruiser ute heading down his driveway.'

'Nah. You know I was crook the other day, barely left my joint. I was laid up in bed.'

'Fair enough. I don't know why this detective is being so hard on you, but keep your head down, yeah? We don't need any more shit coming our way.'

He didn't want to be involved at all in any of this, but knew with the murder next door that every man and their dog were going to come out of the woodwork. It was stress that he didn't need, and he worried just how much more Vanessa could take. He was the level head of the family, the organiser, and he knew just how unpredictable Tom could be, especially now it looked like he was using again.

He had protected him his whole life, and whenever Tom was in a dark place, he would try his best to pick up his workload and lock him away in his trailer, with Vanessa being the only other one who truly knew what was happening with him. He would brush off his absences on the farm to others as bad sickness, but how much longer could he cover for him? The fires and Belle's disappearance seemed to affect him badly, even more than himself and Vanessa, who had both lost so much more.

'Okay,' Tom replied finally.

Arthur braced himself for his next question. And knew it was likely to set his brother off. 'Mate, I know the last few months have been tough, and these coppers on our doorstep are bad news. But, I'm just going to put it out there. Are you using again?'

Tom's face reddened at the accusation. 'Using? Me? Jesus Christ Art, of course not! If you're gonna accuse me of this shit, I may as well just pack up and leave. You don't need me here.'

It was a tactic he would use from time to time. He would threaten to leave, but he and Arthur both knew there was no other place for him. Where would he go? Arthur decided to let his reply sit in the silence for a beat. And he watched as Tom picked at a scab on his left arm, raw and bloody.

'And anyway, what would you do out here without me?! I've been here every bloody day running this joint with ya. You'd be stuffed without me!'

He knew not to push him too hard. He was unpredictable when he used, and he couldn't afford to lose him. 'Fair enough, look I'm not fighting with you, alright? Just keep your head low, ignore these coppers, and whatever you do, don't go talking to them again without telling me, all right?'

'I won't,' he said as he got out and slammed the door in Arthur's face.

Close by, Nick helped Bec and Neville slowly pack away the array of work gear spread across the front of Harry's machinery shed. He watched Bec out of the corner of his eye as she worked, sweating in the hot sun. He was still surprised she had kissed him and he tried to make sense of it. He thought of his life in the city and how busy he was, and for the second time in the last year, wondered if a long-distance relationship could work.

He knew he had tried as hard as he could have with Jemma, his high school sweetheart from home. But she didn't understand his work and the sheer man hours you needed to put in. Maybe Bec would be more accommodating to his busy schedule? All this talk of babies with his sister made him realise he was getting older, and he still wanted to settle down and have kids with the right person. He had just never felt like he had found the right one.

As Bec packed the last clear storage container in the van, he walked over and he asked, 'Walk with me?'

'No worries.'

The two slowly walked past the old shed and into the back paddocks of Harry's farm. He had spent the first half of his life in the bush and felt a comfort in the open land that he could never truly describe. The paddocks were sparse and empty, contrary to the neighbouring properties that had vast rows of orange and mandarin orchards, all blossoming, ready for their next harvest. The sky was a stark blue, and only the slightest whispers of cloud had formed across the horizon. They walked slowly, and in silence, and as they made their way closer to the tree line which formed the back fence of his property, and he finally swallowed his pride and made the first move. 'So, I've been thinking.'

'So have I,' she said.

'You go first.'

She laughed. 'Not a chance, after you.'

'Look, I enjoyed our date the other night, and you make me feel a certain, um, way. Ever since I first met you, I think you feel it too.'

'I do.'

Her answer made him smile. 'Look. I live in Sydney, and you're in Mildura. And I know it's a long way. But I'd like to see where this goes. Maybe you could come to Sydney with me after all of this?'

She looked at him, and the question hung in the air before she replied, 'I would like that.'

She grabbed his left hand and pulled in for a kiss. They stood together under the tree line and for a minute he forgot about everything and just focused on that one moment with her. He held her against his body, and the two stood in the warm, clear country air for what felt like hours, but was only seconds. Just as he was about to pull away, he felt Bec's entire body tense up, and he pulled back quickly and looked into her eyes.

'You okay? What's wrong?'

Her mouth opened twice, but words weren't coming out. She held out her hand and pointed towards the large gum tree directly behind them. He spun around and looked at the tree; It was a huge, sprawling gum tree, and the smooth grey trunk towered above them. At the base of the tree, words were etched deep into the wood.

'Belle.'

Chapter Twenty-Six

By the time Nick had called everyone back to the farm, the sun had begun to set and make its way slowly down past the horizon. He had tasked Pat with bringing the work lights back out onto the farm, and they were soon set up in the back paddock, illuminating the tree line and the tree in question.

He and Maz had stood looking at the base of the trunk, both quiet, in shock at where they could potentially be standing.

'Is this what I think it is?' Maz asked.

Nick ran his fingers over the deep etching on the trunk base. He looked through the tree line, and his senses flared when he realised he could just see the back of Tom Smith's small trailer home from where they stood.

'It could be anything, but look where we are,' he said, pointing over to Tom's home. 'I've read the reports. Police searched the Smith farm. They had dogs, SES, the works.'

Maz nodded. 'And back when that 60 minutes story aired, they had cadaver dogs.'

He remembered back to the tape he'd watched in the police station with her. 'You're right. Surely, they would've been led straight here?'

'Not necessarily. The Smiths are the biggest farm along here, and we are still a couple of hundred metres from their boundary line. If she came from the McKenzie's place and was buried here, they might not have picked up the scent.'

Dogs weren't always as reliable as the shows on TV made them out to be. He knew that from the many missed attempts the K9 unit had had, looking at some of his cases. He knew that farms made things even harder, with the bodies of other small animals, and even fertiliser and pesticides messing up their scents.

As Bec and Neville had begun to re setup all their gear, he noticed a pair of headlights turning in through the McKenzie gate at high speed.

'Who's that?' Maz asked.

'Beats me.'

The car was driving at considerable speed, and as it got closer, he realised it was Vanessa Smith's small hatchback.

She slammed the brakes on around fifty metres before the surrounding police vehicles, and soon the whole group was covered in her dust.

'How did she know we were here?'

'No idea. I'll sort her out,' Maz replied.

Nick heard the door slam and saw her running towards the small digger that Pat had borrowed from the Sexton's farm. Maz walked out to her, and he could hear her yelling. As he approached, she screamed in his direction, and he could see she had been crying. 'What did you find? What did you find? Is it my girl?! What did you find?!'

Maz held her back. 'Ness, please, you've got to give us time. We don't know what we are looking at yet,' Maz replied.

Nick interjected, 'Mrs. Smith, please. We need some time to figure out what we've got here. You will be the first to know if we uncover anything of significance.'

She continued to cry and plead for Maz to get her closer to the tree. Nick didn't need her here when they didn't even know what they had yet. 'Maz, why don't you take her home?'

Maz looked disappointed she was being sent off the scene, but she didn't voice it. 'Of course.'

Once Maz had got Vanessa Smith home and calmed down, she returned and they together watched as Neville and Pat gingerly dug down at the base of the trunk, trying their best to not damage whatever lay beneath the ancient gum tree.

As the hours passed, they had managed to dig a hole three metres wide and two metres deep, taking turns with the shovel in the hard ground and being aided by the Sexton's excavator. Neville advised against the use of the machine to begin with as he didn't want any remains to be damaged, but after a few hours they began to use it, scalloping out larger and larger scoops of earth.

He stepped out of the hole and wiped the sweat off his brow, and shivered. As night had fallen, a cold wind had picked up, and he could see that Maz was shivering as she sipped from her coffee out of her thermos lid.

'What do you think?' she asked.

'I think there's nothing here. Or whatever was here is gone.' He turned back towards Pat and Neville in the hole. Frustrated, he decided to call it. 'Let's pack it up, guys. I don't think we are going to find anything.'

He watched the two men drop the shovels in relief. Neville climbed out of the hole first, and quickly sat down on the ground, taking a swig from a bottle of water. 'I've done some hard yakka in my life, but I might be getting a bit old for this.'

'Why the name here then, detective?' Pat asked, pointing up at the trunk.

Nick looked at the base of the trunk again for about the hundredth time that night. He walked over and slowly bent down and tried to look as close as possible to the etching in the wood. It had been carved neatly, with something extremely sharp, like a knife or chisel, and he could see small pieces of green from the trunk at the base of the words. A thought suddenly came to him, and he kept it to himself for the moment, unsure of whether to play his hand in front of the whole group.

'Who knows? Maybe it was Harry as a young fella? Kids are always scratching things into tree trunks; it could be anything.'

After seeing everyone off and quickly wishing Bec good night, Nick got back to the pub in record time, and was still covered from head to toe in dirt from all the digging. He looked at the time on his phone: 10pm. He hoped he could sneak in one beer before Dan closed up for the night.

He parked behind the pub and walked straight past the door of his caravan, trying his best to brush the last remnants of dirt off his shirt, he walked through the dark back hallway and through the bistro which had shut, and into the front bar, which seemed oddly quiet for a Friday night.

Dan was polishing a glass of beer, with one eye on the cricket on the TV behind the patrons seated on the stools in front of him. He turned around as Nick walked in and came over with an expectant look on his face. 'Anything?'

He assumed Maz had updated him on where she was off to when he called and hoped that the local barman could keep it to himself. The last thing he needed was for half the town, thinking they had found Belle Smith's body.

He shook his head. 'Nothing. We dug down around two metres. It's empty.'

'Bugger. We thought you may have found her.'

'Yeah, I thought we had something. I thought we may have as well.'

He walked up behind the taps and asked, 'Beer?'

'Please.'

He sat quietly, sipping the cold beer, and scrolled through his phone sitting on the bar top. Sometimes he wasn't even looking at anything, but did it because he didn't want to be bothered. He felt the glares of the locals on the back of his head and knew that time was running out. This town needed answers. A few minutes later, he felt a tap on his shoulder. 'Nick?' said the voice from behind him.

Anna Denholm stood behind him, dressed for a night out in dark jeans and a shimmering low-cut top. She wore neat diamond stud earrings and her short hair was tied up into a small ponytail on the top of her head. It was the first time he had seen her wearing makeup, and it was tastefully done, with pale pink lips and the slightest instance of blush. Whoever her ex was must have been an idiot for leaving her, he thought. She was the best-looking woman in Darfield by far.

'Sorry to bother you. I hoped you might be here,' she said with a shy smile.

He guessed she hadn't heard the rumours around town yet and was glad she hadn't. He didn't have the mental capacity after the day he'd had to explain it all to her again. 'No worries at all. You look a little overdressed to be in here with us.'

She blushed. 'Mum's night out, me and a couple of girlfriends went out for dinner in Mildura. I thought I'd stop in before I got back to the shop.' She looked left and right at the other patrons. 'I was hoping we could have a word?'

His curiosity piqued, he replied, 'Of course.' He looked down along the long bar, and then back out towards the darkened bistro. 'Hey Dan, can I grab a bottle of red to go?'

Dan's eyebrows raised at the unlikely pair, and he replied, 'Yeah, sure.'

'Follow me,' Nick said.

He sat on the edge of his bed in the caravan, and Anna sat at the small bench table. The van was tight inside, and he smelt her fruity perfume wafting toward him. He poured them both a glass of red, and took a quick sip, impressed by Dan's taste. Bailey had made a new friend and pushed herself in between Anna and the side wall of the caravan, and soon fell back into a quiet sleep.

'Sorry about this. You never know who's listening in there.'

She smiled. 'It's fine, and you're totally right. There are a lot of gossipers in this town, and I don't want them knowing any more than they have to, although me coming back to your caravan isn't a good look.'

'Yeah, I didn't quite think that one through,' he said with a chuckle. 'You wanted to speak to me?'

Her demeanour changed, and her smile slowly faded. She took a sip from her wineglass, and slowly rocked it round and around the glass base, watching the liquid smoothly loll around inside the glass. 'Yeah. I did.'

'What's up?'

'It's something you said about Tom Smith the other day. You asked me my thoughts about him. I'll be honest, I'd hardly even thought about him since back then. And I've hardly seen him in twenty years. Maybe a couple of times. But when you asked me, it got me thinking and remembering those days a bit more back then.'

She fell quiet again, and Nick didn't fill that silence. He sat patiently and sipped on his wine, waiting for Anna to continue. 'We had a massive row about a month before she disappeared. We used fake IDs to get into the local pub, and Belle ditched me to hook-up with a guy. Maz Rogers caught me in there and kicked me out. I was so embarrassed. I still feel awkward walking through those doors now, and I'm in my late 30s.'

'Who was the guy?' he asked.

'It's not important. Some farmer, I think, I never saw him again.'

'Ok then.'

She sipped from her wine. 'We didn't talk for a few weeks. And then I decided we needed to have it out. We spoke, and I thought things were okay.'

'Her Mum said she seemed a bit quieter in the weeks leading up to her going missing?'

'I don't know about that. We didn't speak.'

'I thought you said you had made up?' he asked.

'We had. And then we went camping with Tom Smith.'

'So? What happened when you went camping?'

'That's the thing, Nick. Nothing happened. We went to Lake Somerstead, we drank, we partied, we laughed, and we came home.'

'So what's the issue, then?'

'Well, after that trip. She never spoke to me again.'

Chapter Twenty-Seven

Anna sat in the passenger seat of the old work ute and held her left arm out the window, feeling the wind rush through her fingers. Tom Smith drove, and Belle sat squished between them, with one leg in her footwell and the other against Tom's, nearly touching the brake pedal.

It had been a weird few weeks between her and Belle after their night out at the pub. When they woke the next morning, Belle was nowhere to be found, presumably packing up and leaving while Anna still slept. She still wasn't quite sure what had happened when she had found her walking away from the pub, and Belle was adamant as they walked home she was fine, which Anna could tell she clearly wasn't. She was still angry that she had left her alone, and that she had to face Maz Rogers alone. Belle had tried to call a couple of times the next week, and had popped into the shop and spoke with Anna's Mum, but Anna wanted her to know she was hurting and needed time before she would talk to her again.

After a week, she finally cooled down enough to talk again and went out to the farm to talk to her best friend. She walked up the steps and opened the front door, which was always unlocked. She headed down the hallway and ran into Ness and Joe, sitting at the kitchen table eating lunch.

'Hey Anna, haven't seen you around for a while. How are you?' Ness said.

Anna assumed Belle hadn't said much about their night out and knew to play coy with her Mum. 'I'm good thanks Mrs. Smith, is Belle home?'

'Yeah, of course, love, I think she's out in the back shed.'

'Thanks.'

She walked on through the kitchen and opened the rear sliding door. It was a scorching hot day, and she could see the shimmering iron of the shed roof in the distance. The backyard behind the house had sparse patches of grass, and an old garden bed running away from the house had feeble attempts to plant roses that were long since dead. She couldn't see Belle in the old shed, but made her way over, and hoped she could explain her feelings in a way that wouldn't upset her best friend.

As she got closer, she found her near the back row of work benches, sweating and concentrating as she tightened the rear axle nut on her little brother's bike. The temperature in the shed was considerably hotter than outside, and she could feel beads of sweat already beginning to drip down her back, even though she was in a light sundress.

'What are you doing?' she asked.

'Bloody bindi's, second flat Joe has had this month.' Belle wiped the sweat off her forehead, and she could see grease marks on her left cheek. 'Dad's been so busy lately, and who knows where Uncle Tom is? Thought I'd just do it myself.'

Belle never ceased to amaze her. Growing up on the farm, she was capable of many tasks that Anna wasn't. She could change bike tyres, she helped her Dad service their machinery, would help out with fencing, and would drive tractors. There wasn't much her headstrong friend wouldn't try, or didn't seem to pick up quickly.

'Fair enough.'

'Hey list..'

Belle cut her off with one hand in her direction. 'No, it's me who should apologise. I don't know what's got into me.'

Anna was on the back foot. She didn't expect Belle to be the one apologising.

Belle continued, 'You're my best friend. I shouldn't have ditched you. I'm sorry.'

She felt tears begin to well up in her eyes, and the tension in the old shed seemed to evaporate in an instant. 'I'm sorry too, Belle. I've been acting like a bit of a bitch. I've been selfish.'

Belle laughed. 'Don't be so hard on yourself An, I may have seemed out of it, but I wanted to go home with him.'

She knew Belle looked older than her, but she never really seemed to show huge amounts of interest in guys. Her answer surprised her, but she knew they were nearly eighteen and it was a sign of things to come.

'I'm sorry. I guess I should've let you go then.'

'It's all good. I got his number.'

Anna was surprised. 'Oh. Wow. Really? How old is he? He wasn't bad looking.'

Belle blushed. 'He's name is Aaron, and he's twenty-four. I know, I know, he's a bit older than us, but we've been talking a little bit. He was really nice.' She wiped her hands on a rag on the bench and walked over to her and hugged her.

'I'm sorry about Maz Rogers. That would've been so awkward for you.'

She laughed. 'Well, I'm eighteen in three months, so not much she can do about it then!'

The two girls laughed together, the last pieces of tension between them gone. As they walked back to the house, Belle stopped. 'Hey, Uncle Tom is going camping down at Lake Somerstead tomorrow night. I know it's been a few years since we've gone with him, but I kind of feel bad. I think he's lonely, he's always asking me. And at least this time he's said we can have a few drinks with him, so shouldn't be too bad. What do you think?'

Anna's mind cast back to her uncle sitting on Belle's bed, and the scent of his work shirt. 'Sounds like fun.'

Back in Tom's ute, he drove down the main state highway and passed a road sign which read, 'Lake Somerstead 10km.' The sun was high in the sky and they had made good time. It was only a 200km drive south of Darfield.

The girls had been adamant they wanted to stop in Mildura, and he didn't feel like fighting with them, plus he needed to make a stop of his own. They pulled into a service station and as the girls ran inside; he made his way into the bathrooms and after checking the coast was clear, locked himself in the disabled toilets.

Closing the lid and sitting down, he unrolled the small foil bag he had in his top shirt pocket. His skin had itched for the entire drive. He knew he was using too much, but with the amount that was being dropped at the farm, who would even notice? He carefully took two small shards and placed them into the bowl of his glass pipe, and put it up to his lips, carefully running the open flame from his lighter up and back under the bowl, watching the meth crystallise and turn into vapour.

He felt the burning sensation enter his lungs and held it down for as long as possible. He had smoked pot forever, and after years of abuse, he felt like it no longer had any effect on him except making him tired. He had started popping the odd ecstasy pill when they were busy on the farm, but they made him sweat terribly, and Arthur had begun to notice. When a supplier who had come to drop off more product had offered him a smoke of his pipe, he felt an immediate draw to it, and knew he could keep himself straighter by smoking this instead of the pills.

He exhaled and watched the small room slowly fill with the acidic smoke. He felt his skin come alive and could feel a warm tingling sensation begin at the base of his spine, slowly creep up his back and across his shoulder blades like a warm hug. He thought of the girls back at the ute, and about Belle's long tanned leg, resting against his on the drive here. His little niece was now a woman. And it wasn't like they were blood related; he thought. Who knows what the weekend might bring?

Back in the ute, he sat and waited and watched the two girls come out of the servo with snacks, both laughing. Anna walked in front of Belle and was wearing short denim shorts and a crop top which left a lot for his imagination, and he eyed her body with greed, the drugs making him think bad thoughts about both of the girls now.

Anna flicked water out of the bucket beside the petrol bowser at Belle and laughed as the soapy water went all down the front of Belle's top.

'Ugh, you bitch!' Belle yelled in her direction.

'Oh, don't be such a sook, you love it.'

'You want to swap seats? My legs are longer than yours.'

Anna looked over at the ute and at Tom sitting in the driver's seat. 'Is your uncle okay? He seems a bit quieter than usual?'

Belle squinted in the sunlight in the ute's direction. 'Oh really? Nah, seems fine to me. He's a bit like Dad in a way, sometimes you can't shut him up and sometimes he's quiet.'

She hoped she hadn't said anything wrong to him and looked forward to having a drink with him that night, maybe even after Belle had gone to bed. 'Yeah, I'll take the middle,' she replied, secretly happy they would be sitting so close for the remainder of the trip.

When they got to the lake, they drove slowly down the gravel road that led to the caravan park which sat against it. It looked busy with people setting up for the long weekend. Tents and caravans in neat rows lined the shoreline, and ski boats sat in the cool water, ready for the weekend adventures. There was a kiosk at the caravan park, and Anna remembered Belle and her visiting it as kids, buying ice creams and lollies and more worms for Tom to fish with.

'We camping in the same spot as usual?' she asked Tom, who was focusing forward on the road.

'Not this time An, I've heard there's a good spot out on Cove Point.'

Anna felt Belle's shoulder drop. They knew Cove Point. It was nearly on the other side of the lake, and it wasn't walking distance back to the kiosk. They would need a lift to get back to civilization.

'Fair enough,' she replied.

When they finally got to the other side of the lake to Cove Point, they came to a small campground that had lush green grass running down to the lake line. The sun had just begun to lower itself in the sky, and it looked like they only had a couple of hours of light left. The weather was perfect for a swim, Anna thought, but they decided to get their campsite ready first, and busied themselves with pulling out three small tents, and setting up a small gazebo to protect themselves from the sun and wind.

Once they were finally set up, the eskys were opened, and Anna's eyes widened at the amount of alcohol Tom had bought. 'Don't tell your Mum and Dad,' he said, winking in her direction. She blushed as she watched him take his shirt off. Standing in the sunlight, she looked at his tanned body and his thick chest hair and was excited to see what the night would bring.

After they had all had a swim, they sat on the riverbank and decided to sunbake. She looked at her watch; it was only four. She was already on her second drink and, combined with the sun, could already feel it going to her head.

Belle drank from her bottle and flicked her long, blond hair over her shoulders. 'God, this stuff is good. I've never tried the watermelon flavour.' She pulled a cigarette out of her handbag and offered Anna one.

'Thanks,' she said, taking the lighter.

Hours later, the sun had set, and the party had really started. Tom had forgotten food, so the girls only had their snacks from the service station to eat. Listening to pop music, the girls danced beside the fire, singing and laughing, and he was happy to see them still in their bikini tops. He had snuck away earlier and smoked a little more, and the warmth of the fire hit him in waves, rising from his toes to the tip of his head.

The girls were still laughing, and they both popped themselves down on either side of him, cracking their next drinks.

'So, you girls having fun?' he asked.

'Much more fun than anything at home,' Anna said, smiling in his direction.

As he drank more and more, the alcohol was mixing with the meth; and he felt like he knew where the night was taking him. He was going to wait until Belle went to her tent, and he was going to have a crack at Anna. She was nearly eighteen, and he had seen the way she looked at him. He knew she wanted him.

The night wore on, and he could see the girls were both getting drunk. Belle danced by herself at the fire, slowly to the music, and Anna sat on the nearby log, smiling in his direction. She looked ripe for the taking, he thought, and he decided to sneak off and have one last hit before he tried his luck.

'Back in a minute,' he said in Anna's direction over the music.

'See you soon,' she said with a bleary-eyed smile.

He headed back behind the bush and smoked the last bit of his stash for his trip, feeling the warmth wash over him once again. He felt like Superman as he walked back to the fire, and there was nothing but the tiniest glimpse of flame holding him straight. Looking around, it looked like he had taken a bit longer than he thought, and both the girls had already made their way to bed.

He stumbled towards his chair and barely managed to pull his bottle from the cup holder; he looked over at the two tents and his lone swag beside his ute and smiled at his options.

She might fight a bit. The last one did as well. He loved them when they were like that.

He crept over to Anna's tent and couldn't hear a peep coming from either of the tents. Silently, he opened the zipper and made his way inside. It was pitch black dark and he couldn't see in front of him, but he ran his arm up the warm leg and felt himself getting aroused. He made his way up to where he thought her face was and quickly held his hand over her mouth, feeling her tense up as she woke.

Anna was passed out silently in the tent beside them. Blissfully unaware of what was about to happen to her best friend.

Chapter Twenty-Eight

Nick and Anna had finished the bottle of wine together the night previous and he had used every shred of mental willpower in him to not make a move. He had had many partners in the past and none had truly seemed to stick, but he truly wanted to try to make things work with Bec.

He had awoken later than usual, with a splitting headache. He was never much of a wine drinker and was now feeling the effects of drinking half a bottle. He searched through his bag and found one lonely Panadol tablet; it'll have to do for now, he thought. As he was reading his texts from Bec from the night before, his phone rang in his hand.

'Morning. I tried to knock this morning. Were you out?' Maz asked.

'Ahh no. Might have slept in a bit.'

'It's been one of those weeks. You needed it. Dan said you had a visitor?' she asked curiously.

He decided to cut straight through the rumour; he didn't need Bec hearing anything. 'I did. Anna Denholm, she came to give me some information.'

'Oh, did she now?'

'She did. I'll meet you down at the station in twenty.'

He quickly showered and brushed his teeth, hoping it would wash away his terrible red wine breath. He was a beer drinker, and wine always went straight to his head and the hangover felt like someone had swung an axe right between his eyes. He gagged slightly as he rinsed out his mouth and knew it was going to be a long day.

It was a beautiful, clear, crisp morning in Darfield, and he decided to make the short trip over to the police station on foot. He needed the time anyway to compose a short email to the Chief. All of the leading detectives did it this way he knew, phone calls for good news and emails for bad. At least he felt like he may have a lead with this fake ID, after his chat with Anna last night.

Chief,

Possible grave site found on McKenzie farm. I'm sure media will be all over it by now. Nothing found as yet. Have a couple of leads I'm following up. Anything bites and you'll be the first to know.

DS Vada.

Reading the email back to himself, he realised he pretty much had nothing, and wondered how much longer the Chief would keep him out here for. He was a handy resource at the Chief's disposal, and the Chief knew better than anyone when that resource was being wasted. He sent the email off and knew that the Chief would see straight through it; he needed more time here, and he wasn't sure if he was going to get it. As he passed by the local school, his phone rang again, an unknown number this time.

'Hello?'

'Good morning Detective Vada, this is Hannah Jones from Channel Four news. We are hearing reports of a possible grave site, discovered on the McKenzie farm. Can you confirm this?'

Here we go again, he thought. 'I'm unable to comment at this time, Miss Jones. When we know more, we will let everybody know. How did you get this number? Please don't call it again.'

He hung up before she could reply. Reporters had somehow got his number from time to time in the past, and he felt them more of a hindrance than a help. Walking into the police station, most of the same crew was inside as yesterday. Maz took centre stage, with her feet on the desk and a cigarette in hand.

'Morning Sergeant.'

'Morning all. What have I missed?'

'I was just saying that, with your permission, of course, I'd like to head out to Harry's home and have a look around,' Prue said.

He thought about the media sniffing around the property, and the sight of Prue Thornton leading a police search. It'd be pandemonium with the media, and he didn't need anything else going wrong. He knew, however, her insight into Harry's last few days could be invaluable, and he decided to give her a shot.

'It's a good idea,' he said, as he watched Maz's eyebrows shoot up. 'Another set of eyes wouldn't hurt. I'll take you out there myself. I've only got one condition.'

'What's that?' she asked.

He smiled. 'That you stay low on the drive out. If the media sees me and you in the car, they'll have a field day.'

She chuckled. 'Sounds good to me.'

Maz cleared her throat. 'So, you said you had news?'

He sat down at the table beside her. 'I do.'

He laid out his last two conversations with Anna. The camping trip, how Belle hadn't spoken to Anna afterward, and the fake IDs.

'Well, that explains that then,' Maz said finally, after Nick was done.

'What?'

'Her in the pub back then. I caught her coming out of the ladies' bathrooms. God knows how Dan didn't recognise her. The pub was much busier on Saturday nights back then. We'd hired a bouncer, his name was Jerry, who would come man the door on busy nights to help us out. I took one look at her and knew she was underage. Obviously, I knew who she was, but I never knew anything about fake IDs. I wondered how she'd got past him.'

'And Belle.'

'Yes, and Belle. I can't speak for that. I never saw her there.'

Prue had sat listening to their conversation intently and piped up. 'I tried to talk to Anna for the podcast, but she always declined. I wish I had known about this sooner.' She opened her laptop on her lap and started to type furiously. 'Their fake IDs. Did Anna say if it was their names on them?'

'I asked that. Brittany Reardon was the name on Belle's.'

'What about Anna's?'

'No idea, didn't ask.'

'Brittany Reardon.' Prue let the name sit in the quiet room. 'Doesn't ring any bells.'

'Maz, Let's put out a nationwide alert on the name Brittany Reardon. It was a NSW driver's licence. Who knows? Maybe there's something out there relating to it. Someone might have found the old card?'

'I'm going to do my own research, see what I can find,' Prue replied as she typed. 'And what about this camping trip? What happened there?'

'I think we need to look closer at Tom Smith. This whole camping trip is fishy. Why would Belle stop talking to Anna after it? What happened out there?'

'Sam and I are heading back out to Belgrove to update Vanessa. How about we pay Tom Smith another visit while you check out Harry's with Prue?' Maz asked.

'Good idea, give me a call if he's causing any trouble.'

The morning sun tried its hardest to break through the thick cloud cover as they made their way back out towards the McKenzie farm, and Prue slowly filled in Nick with her life story as he drove. He hadn't eaten breakfast, which was a mistake, and although the morning was cool, he could feel damp sweat on his brow, the last remnants of the red wine trying to escape his body.

As they approached the gates to the McKenzie farm, they looked at the now busy entrance. News vans lined both sides of the gravel road and a lone reporter and camera man stood metres into the front paddock. With the farmhouse in the distance, he could see her positioning herself for the best angle. The media were a necessary evil in his profession, and they could be used to his advantage from time to time, but sometimes the intensity was too much for him.

She lowered herself down silently into the footwell of the police car, just in time for multiple cameras to swing in his direction as he made the turn through the gates a lot quicker than he usually would. He managed to shower half of the camera crews in dust as they tried to get a good view of who was in the car, and he heard some swear words at his entrance.

After deciding to leave Harry's home office until last, they slowly worked their way through each room one by one. Prue busied herself in the kitchen, going through drawer by drawer, unsure of what she was searching for. Nick finished in the bedroom and sat on the edge of Harry's bed. Absolutely nothing of note. The house was extremely clean considering it had had doors left open for multiple days, and Nick wondered if Harry was slightly obsessive compulsive. He'd never seen a farmhouse like it, glass windows polished, with hardly a speck of dust on any surface. Even his shirts were colour coded in the cupboards and drawer faces in his walk-in robe labelled.

He walked back into the kitchen to Prue. 'Nothing.'

'Same here.'

'I'll have to give it to the bloke; he was a clean freak.'

Prue laughed. 'To the point of obsession. He came to my house in Melbourne for his podcast interview. Within five minutes, he was vacuuming and organising my drawers. You couldn't stop him.'

Nick always found it funny how, in his profession, he would find out the small idiosyncrasies of a victim when speaking to their friends and loved ones. Each one would be a small piece that ultimately formed their personality, and always helped when he tried to get in the mind of the victim.

'Let's try the office.'

They made their way down to the home office and noted the only thing missing in there was the computer tower, which had been sent off for forensic analysis. It was as neat and tidy as the rest of the house, and he sat down in the office chair to look over the many maps spread across the wall.

Prue went to the wall and slowly ran her fingers across it, stopping at each face in the images. Below the map was a list of towns that had each been crossed out. 'Mt Isa, Mildura, Bathurst, Deniliquin, Longreach, Cradock, what does this mean?' Prue asked.

He surveyed the map and the names of towns below it. Harry was clearly on the trail of someone. Had he been looking for Belle's kidnapper? Or killer?

'No idea. Looks like he was searching for something, or someone.'

Looking under the desk, there were two filing cabinets on each side. He bent down and tried to open both, and found they were both locked.

'Both locked, any ideas?'

'Give me a sec,' she said as she ran out of the room and was back within a minute, holding a pair of small black plastic keys. 'Was in the cutlery drawer in the kitchen.'

He unlocked both cabinets and wasn't surprised to see them jam packed with files, and neatly ordered with typed labels indicating what was what. He ran his fingers through each tab in the left cabinet. It showed mostly insurance company names, some he had heard of and some he hadn't. The right-hand side cabinet was much more fruitful and, getting to the first tab, it read, 'Belle Smith.'

He pulled out the entire file, separated half the paper inside, and handed it to Prue, who he could see eyes had lit up. She went back out to the dining room and grabbed a spare chair, setting it up on the right-hand end of the desk. She started to read through the papers with excitement.

'Arthur Smith's criminal record, Tom Smith's criminal record, the forensic report from the house one week after the fires. I have all of this; I've seen it all before.'

She looked over at Nick, whose eyes had widened at what he was reading. He started handing pages over to her, and she too soon fell quiet as she read through the information.

'The towns. He was searching. He was searching for her.'

'I think he wasn't telling you the whole story, Prue. I think Harry believed she was still alive.'

Chapter Twenty-Nine

Maz and Sam sat at the dining table with Arthur and Vanessa. Vanessa had been crying, but from where Maz was sitting, she could tell they were more tears of relief than anything.

Arthur was irritated, and she could see it. He sat silently with a scowl and hadn't said a word the whole time Maz had explained the last few days. Vanessa wiped the last of her tears away. 'Thank you Maz. It's such a relief. I thought the worst. I thought you had found her.'

'If you don't mind me asking,' Arthur said. 'If you guys did such a thorough search back then, how did you not find this?'

'We are human, Arthur, I'm sure you can understand. You know as much as anyone we haven't stopped looking for her, and we won't until she is found. Or we know what happened to her.'

Her reply seemed to appease him enough to fall back into silence. She knew the next line of questioning would be tricky, and knew she needed to tread lightly. 'Before I go, I'd like to ask a few more questions.'

'Of course,' Vanessa replied.

'Detective Vada has been interviewing multiple witnesses from back around the time of the fires and he seems to agree with your assumption Vanessa that Belle seemed a bit quieter in the weeks leading up to her disappearance, do you have any idea why she was that way?'

Vanessa looked perplexed at the question. 'No, like I said, I observed it too. She was always a quieter kid, much quieter than Joe. She and Anna had had a falling out over god knows what. I couldn't keep up with them. Teenage girls, you know how it is. I assumed she was just sulking over that.'

'And what's this got to do with her disappearance?' Arthur asked.

'We've been told in the weeks leading up to it that she and Anna went camping with your brother, Tom? Is that correct?'

Arthur smashed both hands down on the table, causing Sam and Vanessa to jump at the outburst. Maz held herself steady and tried to remain cool. 'For fuck's sake, Maz!

There's a shallow grave on the McKenzie farm with my daughter's name written on it! And you're still trying to pin it on my brother! What does he have to do to prove to you he had nothing to do with it!'

'I'd ask you to please remain calm, Arthur. We are doing our best to search every possible avenue on this, which I'm sure you can understand. We currently have people on the farm right now still looking, so we haven't ruled anything out.'

Vanessa turned and placed her hand on Arthur's. 'Calm down, love. You know she's just trying to do her job.'

Arthur pulled his hand out from underneath Vanessa's. 'I've had enough of this. Some of us have work to do.' And with that, he stormed out of the room, slamming the glass sliding door behind him.

Vanessa's eyes followed him out the door, and she looked solemnly back at the two police officers. 'He can be a hot head, which I'm sure you both know, along with the whole of Australia. But he's loyal, and he's never lied to me. But one of his biggest faults is his brother. Sometimes I feel like I'm an outsider to their relationship.'

'I understand that,' Sam said. 'I have four sisters and I would do anything to protect them.'

'This camping trip.' Vanessa asked. 'What's so interesting about it? He took Belle and Anna away plenty of times. How was this any different?'

Maz realised that they were reaching. And by telling Arthur, Tom would know soon enough, which really limited her surprise factor in questioning him.

'It may not have been any different at all. We don't know anything more than you, Vanessa. But what we do know is that her mood change seemed to coincide with the trip. Perhaps she and Tom argued? We can't be sure. But she never spoke again to Anna after that trip.'

'Her and Anna? Are you sure?' She closed her eyes and seemed to let the information wash over her. 'I didn't know that. That is odd.'

'It could be nothing, but we're trying our best to work out timelines. And we'd love to chat with Tom as well if he's around?'

She sipped her cup of tea with a blank expression, still processing what she was hearing. 'I don't think he's home. Pretty sure Arthur sent him into town to get some steel to repair one of the back fences.'

'No worries, we'll call him and arrange a time for another chat.'

'Oh, don't you worry, I'll be chatting with him as well.'

The two officers left shortly after, and only just managed to miss Arthur's hasty exit from the main shed. He had left the house in a fury and walked down to his machinery shed. He took long, deep breaths and tried to clear his mind. He had had trouble with his temper for years; he knew it, and Vanessa knew it. He had tried to hide it from his kids when they were younger, but they too would walk around on eggshells, afraid to see their father in one of his moods. He thought of his brother and the scabs up his arm, and Maz Rogers telling them that Belle had seemed to change after the last camping trip.

He could hardly remember before the fires. The years had formed into blurs when the kids were younger, and he had been busy helping the Sexton's prep for seeding in the weeks leading up to Belle's disappearance and he struggled to remember a change in her demeanour and was disappointed in himself for not being a more attentive parent.

He pulled his phone out and called Tom. He knew he should warn him that the police may come down to his place. Who knew what else he had been lying about? He looked down towards the back of the property in the direction of his house and saw a black car parked near the front of it. That was odd, he thought. Tom rarely had visitors there these days.

He listened to the phone ring a couple of times and then heard him answer. 'Art! You gotta' get up here!'

He tensed up immediately, hearing his brother in distress. 'Tom, what's wrong?' he said as the phone cut out. He thought he had heard a scuffle in the background and the smash of glass. He made a beeline for the gun safe at the back of the old shed and pulled out the closest rifle within arms-reach. Running back and getting into his ute, he accelerated hard towards the house at the back of the farm.

As he flew down the main road which linked the main house to his little brothers, his mind immediately went to their days when they were storing the drugs, and he immediately assumed that whatever was happening in that small house was to do with his brother using again.

He wanted to protect him, but at what cost? Had Tom had something to do with Belle's disappearance? It wasn't even worth thinking of, and he shook his head a couple of times to push the bad thoughts to the back of his mind.

He arrived at the trailer in record time and found a shining black, low slung wagon parked out the front with both doors open. He opened his door slowly and grabbed the rifle off the passenger seat and held it, pointing down to the ground. He cocked the bolt back and flicked off the safety. He had hardly touched guns since he moved to the farm and left the shooting to his brother, but feeling the warmth of the rifle stock in his hands gave him a sense of power he hadn't felt since he ran the streets in Melbourne when he was a young man. He listened out for what was happening inside and could hear Tom's cries from where he stood; and he began to walk over to the front deck and braced himself for what he was about to see.

He put his ear to the door and listened in. 'Please, I don't know what happened to it!' Tom yelled out.

A deeper accented voice came from near the door. 'Listen, if you don't tell us what happened to it, you won't be the last person we hurt on this farm.'

Arthur had heard enough, and although he knew he was a much older man these days, he knew his years of hard work on the farm hadn't weakened him, and he swiftly kicked the trailer door open with as much force as he could muster, almost smashing it back off its hinges.

Walking inside with the rifle held steady, he came across his brother, with his hands tied behind his back, sitting on his kitchen chair. Two hulking European men stood between them, both with thick black beards. One had tattoos all over his neck, right to his chin, and had a menacing glare. The other was shorter and had his hair tied back in a ponytail. He held a knife in his right hand and calmly smiled back at him. In a thick accent, he spoke, 'So, you must be the famous Arthur Smith? You're smaller than what they said.'

Who the hell were these guys? And why were they in his brother's trailer? Tom looked badly hurt, and he knew he had to buy some time. 'How about you put that knife down and we'll talk?'

He looked at Tom and could see he had taken the beating of his life. His left eye had closed up and he had blood gushing from his left knee. The men stood still, and both looked ready for action. Arthur knew he had to show them who was boss and in a split second decision, cocked the rifle back and shot at the floor between them both.

The gunshot noise was like an explosion in the small trailer, and both of the men jumped instinctually away from the bullet. He heard Arthur whimper and he could feel his own ears ringing as he yelled, 'I'm not fucking around!'

The smaller man of the two lowered the knife onto the ground and held both hands up in defeat. 'Okay, okay. The knife's down. Now we talk.'

'What do you want?'

'We want our product back. All of it.'

He was confused. They hadn't had product on the property for more than five years. He had told Tom he didn't want anything to do with it anymore, that it was getting too risky. 'What do you mean? We don't store anything here for you anymore?'

The man smiled. 'I'm not sure your brother is telling you the whole story.'

He looked at his brother, who had a crestfallen look on his face, and had begun to cry. 'Please, just kill me. I don't want to be here anymore.'

'Tom … What did you do?'

Tom tried to wipe his face and cursed when he realised he was tied up. Through quiet sobs, he spoke, 'I knew the farm was struggling. You would tell me all the time. These guys are just using us. Why shouldn't we take a piece of cake as well?'

He was putting two and two together as his brother spoke, and realised they were in much worse trouble than he first thought.

The shorter man confirmed it. 'Your brother has been storing our stock for years. And now he's been selling it from underneath us. There are only two bags left from the ten we dropped the other month.'

His heart fell. His brother had kept storing the drugs on the farm without his knowledge. And was selling from underneath his nose, and from what he could tell, using as well. From what Tom explained to him when the deal was first setup all those years ago was that these guys were extremely bad people. Much more organised and lethal than the groups they had involved themselves with when they were young men.

He watched the second man of the two closely and could see him beginning to tense up. He cocked the bolt action on his rifle back and forth again and pointed it at his chest. 'You move once more and I'll fuckin' shoot ya.' The man glared back at him but stood deathly still. 'Okay, so how can we fix this?' he asked.

'We want our product back.'

'Why don't I just shoot both of you now and bury you out in my paddock?'

The man held both of his hands up, surrendering. 'Fair enough. We don't have a problem with you. It's your brother who owes us.'

'Well, you're on my property, so if you don't get the fuck off it in the next five minutes, the next bullet won't miss.'

He knew while he had the gun; he had the power, and they both looked at each other and made the decision to leave. The shorter man looked down at Tom, who was still tied to the dining chair. 'I'm sure you will see us again.'

They both then turned and calmly walked past Arthur and back down the steps of the old deck. Arthur watched as they both hopped back inside the wagon and drove away out the way they had come in.

Arthur turned and looked at his brother in the chair. He grabbed a knife from the cutlery drawer and cut the ties from his hands.

'Art, I can explain.'

'Don't,' he replied, holding a hand up. 'Do you realise how fucked you are? I don't want any part of this! You kept storing this shit! When I told you we needed to stop! You owe them the money, and I'm not helping you. You've really fucked yourself, mate.'

Tom held his knee with both hands, trying to stem the blood loss. 'Help me Art, my knee is really bad, I think I need to go to a hospital.'

'There is no way you are going to a hospital!' He threw a tea towel on his lap. 'Wrap it up with that, and don't you fucking dare leave this house.'

Tom pleaded, 'We'll figure it out. We always do.'

'No mate. I figure it out. I do! All you do is fuck things up!' He was seething now; he had moved out here to get away from all of his problems of the past. 'I came here out here to get away from all of the shit. And you've brought it here with us! Stay the hell away from us. I'm not having you bring this shit down on Vanessa. I didn't want a part of it from the start. We were finally starting to get ahead, and you've gone and fucked it all up.' He was disgusted with his younger brother and shook his head as he walked towards the door. He turned back and said, 'Honestly, I hope they kill you.'

Tom sat silently and his head swam, his whole leg was screaming in agony and he was sure they had hit an artery, he hoped the towel would stem the blood loss, but he could still see it seeping between his fingers, making a puddle on the floor. He knew that his actions would come back to bite him, but with the amount he was using lately, it just hadn't seemed like the suppliers were going to be that big of a problem. It was something that he thought he could solve later.

And then his brother asked him something he never hoped he would never ever ask. 'And also, the coppers were back again today. They were asking about some camping trip you went on with Belle and Anna? What's that all about?'

Chapter Thirty

Nick sat back at the police station. They had dragged three of the desks together to form a large meeting table and had spread information across it from end to end, and all the team had assembled back together to provide an update to him.

'We've spent the last day out at the back of the McKenzie's. We haven't found a thing, no physical evidence in the ground. We dug three metres on either side of the hole we dug the other day. Nothing at all,' Neville said.

'Good work. I think we can now safely assume that there is nothing there. Who knows why the names on that tree? She may have done it as a kid?'

'I guess we'll never know,' Maz replied. 'How did you go at the house?'

He smiled. 'Nothing of substance except in the study. We got into the filing cabinet thanks to Prue.' He laid the folder of papers down in front of Maz. 'Have a read of these.'

Maz slid the glasses from her nose upwards and quietly read through the documents. He watched her eyes widen in confusion as she got to the end. 'Hang on. So, from what I'm reading here, Harry thought she was still alive?'

'It certainly looks that way,' he replied.

'I don't get it,' Sam said. 'Why would she run away? She had her whole life ahead of her?'

'I knew her, Nick. She was a good kid. She wouldn't have done that to her family, or Anna,' Maz said to him.

'Where would she have gone, though?' Prue asked. 'She was the most recognisable face in the nation, for a few years at least. There would've been tipoffs, surely.'

'She wouldn't have got far, that's for sure,' he said. He leant back in his chair and rubbed at his temples in frustration. 'So we have no hit's on the fake ID, no hit's on the ute Arthur saw, and Vanessa and Arthur didn't know anything about the camping trip.'

'Basically, we have nothing.' Prue said finally to the group.

Maz stood up first. 'Well, I don't know about you guys, but I'm calling it for the day. I've tried calling Tom Smith twice, Nick. Nothing yet.'

'I'll try him as well. I think he's the key to all of this.'

The group slowly got up, and each left on their own accord, leaving only Bec and Nick still sitting at the big table. She smiled in his direction and said, 'Well, there's no more crime scenes for me to look at today. How about we take the afternoon off?'

He rarely switched off, but the endless days of dead ends were finally starting to get to him. He looked at Bec sitting at the table in her navy-blue police jumpsuit and couldn't believe a woman so beautiful could be a police officer.

He smiled. 'Why not?'

Arthur had left Tom's home soon after the two suppliers had, and Tom sat on his couch in excruciating pain. He took the towel off his knee to look at the wound and could tell they had hit a nerve or artery. The pain was so fierce that he could feel nausea passing over him in waves. He deserved this; he thought to himself, as he looked down at the mess. He had lost a lot of blood going by the pool underneath him, and he knew his time was up.

He'd managed to move from the dining chair to his lounge with much difficulty and grabbed the warm beer bottle from the side table beside him and took a swig. Reaching over into the top drawer of the side table, he grabbed his glass pipe and began the routine of packing it one last time.

He had fobbed off Art's attempts to ask him what had happened back then on that camping trip and he had left in a rage. He knew his feeble excuses that he gave him wouldn't last for long. He had played the night over and over in his mind many times throughout his life and felt a deep shame for what he had done. Whenever he used it slid towards the back of his mind, and the pain and guilt of what he had done stayed there. It was when he was sober, when the demons would return, and shortly after, he'd find himself back where he started and used again.

His idea to carve Belle's name on the tree had been made in a panic. After Maz and the detective had interviewed him, he had racked his mind for ways to throw them off his scent. With all of this heat now, he knew he had to think outside the box, and a few nights earlier, snuck out and scratched his niece's name into the base of the biggest tree on Harry's farm. It was a long shot, but the police found it even quicker than he had thought and had busied themselves digging up half of his paddock.

Killing McKenzie was a mistake, he knew that now, but he knew that in time he would've learned the truth about the camping trip, and before long would've reported it to the police. His constant barrages of questions about that time back then whenever he saw him had finally come to a head, and when he accused him of abusing Belle, he had snapped and shot Harry in a fit of rage. Planting Belle's old school uniform had been an afterthought, and he had only done it the day after he shot Harry, hoping it may confuse the police.

Finishing the contents of the pipe, he felt tears streaming down his cheek as he struggled to stay conscious from the blood loss. He knew he had to end it. There was no turning back now. He had lost his brother, and he knew the cops would soon find out he had killed Harry. They were never going to stop.

He reached back into his drawer and pulled out the old .22 pistol his father had given him as a boy. It stayed in that drawer fully loaded, and there had been many times he had got it out over the years when it all got too hard, and he toyed with the idea of ending it.

Chapter Thirty-One

Bec had brought a change of clothes with her that day as she was staying out of town, but Nick had to pop back to the caravan to change into something more casual. Once they were both ready, they got back into his police car and turned onto the main highway, leading back toward Mildura.

Nick had passed a couple of small boutique wineries on his way to Darfield, and passed his phone over to Bec, and told her to pick one. 'Trentham Hills, Red Cliffs, Gill Estate,' she read out loud. 'Any preferences?'

'As long as they have food. And good beer I'll be happy.'

'Right, Ludlam Valley. They have wine and beer on tap, and a restaurant.'

'Sound good to me.'

As he drove on the main highway, past the turnoff to Belgrove and the McKenzie farm, he felt guilty for taking time away from the case. He was an obsessive worker, sometimes to a fault, and was told by many partners that he was incapable of switching off. When he did finally switch off, he found himself bored, and when he was bored, he drank. He had tried his best to curb his habit over the last year and had stayed the course so far, only drinking on the odd occasion, but a chance to drink with a gorgeous woman he was never going to pass up.

Nick sat in the picturesque vineyard with Bec and couldn't shake the feeling that something wasn't right. He tried to put the feeling to the back of his mind and focus on Bec as she leaned back and let the sun wash over her face. 'It's beautiful here, much nicer than Edithvale,' she said.

The winery was set in a low valley, and the vineyard flowed on from the outdoor seating area they sat in, down to the lowest point of the farm. The place was busy, and couples of all different ages sat laughing and enjoying the beautiful weather. The wine was flowing, and the food was great. But Nick was troubled. He couldn't stop thinking about Harry's office, all the maps, and of his search for Belle. What had changed his line of thinking? What had made him think she was alive? He had the case file and had read it over and over; the evidence pointed to her either being kidnapped or murdered; she had vanished without a trace. What did he know that he didn't?

'Yeah, certainly a lot greener as well,' he said finally.

Bec looked at him with concern. 'Are you ok?'

'Yeah, I'm fine, I'm sorry. I know you wanted us to get away and forget. But I just can't switch off sometimes.'

She looked at him and smiled. 'I get it. When you're out here and you're in charge, I can see that it bears on you. You need to remember that everyone else is here to help. We're not against you. You need to try not to do it all yourself.'

He thought about most of his major cases and realised that most of the time he had made a break; it had been alone. He usually preferred to work alone, as the outside noise and thoughts of others often distracted him. Belle Smith's disappearance had shocked the nation, and from the minute he arrived in Darfield, all he could think about was if he was the one to solve it, and the repercussions that could have for his career. He wasn't sure if he wanted to give up being a detective quite yet, with the internal politicking at head office often making his head ache. Some of the things his Chief had told him about others climbing up the ranks made him think sometimes whether it was really all worth it, and whether he should just focus on his detective work and not try to climb the ladder.

'I know. Sometimes it all just gets too much, and I need to be alone. I've always been a bit of a loner, I guess. I work better by myself.'

He sipped from the cold beer and watched the light grey clouds slowly begin to cover the sun, covering the outdoor area in shadowy darkness. He felt like the clock was ticking. He was either going to end up back at home with nothing to show or have all the answers within the next few days. They continued drinking and slowly worked their way through two plates of beautiful food. His tastes were still very bland due to growing up on meat and two veggies for most of his upbringing, but he always promised himself to try to be more adventurous when he moved to the city, and slowly nibbled on the salty Greek cheese Bec had offered him.

'Wow, this is amazing! What is it?'

Bec chuckled. 'It's saganaki.'

Nick let the word roll off his tongue. 'Saganaki, I don't mind it.'

Suddenly, his phone shrilled loudly in the quiet outdoor area. Looking down, it showed another private number. He let it go to voicemail, hoping to not be bothered by reporters for one afternoon. As he flipped it over on the table, he felt it vibrate again, and cursed under his breath as he answered. 'Listen, I'm no..'

Maz Rogers interrupted him. 'Nick, where are you?'

'I'm in Mildura, at Ludlam Valley with Bec. What's up?'

'Just had reports of gunshots out at the Smith's, I'm about to head out.'

Nick tensed up and knew his feelings had been correct. Something was happening. He just wasn't quite what yet. 'Hold tight. We're 40 minutes away. We'll meet you there.'

Bec had watched his expression as he spoke on the phone and had a look of concern. 'Who was that?'

'Maz Rogers. Gunshots at Smiths, we need to leave. Now.'

They quickly got up and went and sorted out their bill. Nick could feel the effects of the few beers as he started up his car.

'Are you ok to drive?' Bec asked.

'I'll be fine.'

They raced towards the farm and made the entrance to the property in record time. Pat and Sam had parked their vehicles across the front gate and two media vans were parked down by the roadside. Seeing the police cars, they sensed a story, and they were probably right, he thought. Pat moved the police vehicle back to allow for their car to get through and he could see one of the reporters clamouring to get to them, holding a recorder out.

He stopped and wound his window down to speak with Pat. 'Maz is already up at the house. She told us to close off the front gates to keep this lot out,' Pat said.

'Thanks mate.'

'No dramas. You guys stay safe up there. Maz thinks it might be a suicide.'

He wound the window up and let that thought sit in his head. Why would any of the Smiths even consider suicide?

Arriving at the house, Maz's police car was parked out front, and the driver's side door was left ajar. He slowed down beside it and looked over to Bec. 'I need you to stay in the car and get down low. I can't afford to see someone else I care about get hurt.'

Bec shook her head. 'I'm coming with you; you're going to need all the help you can get.'

They didn't have time to continue the conversation as Maz came out of the front door of the home, and met them at the bonnet of the car. She looked frazzled, and for the first time he had ever seen, was wearing her bulletproof flak jacket. 'Gunshots out at Tom's. Ness is locked up inside now. I'm going to get Sam up here to keep an eye on her.'

Nick raced to the boot of his vehicle and slipped on his flak jacket as well. He grabbed his pistol from the small case and checked the rounds in the clip.

'I'll stay here and keep an eye out as well?' Bec asked.

'Great idea,' he said, glad their argument was now solved. He knew she would be in less danger being back inside the house.

'C'mon, let's go.'

They jumped inside her police vehicle and raced towards the back of the farm; his senses were now on high alert as Maz filled him in on what she believed had gone down. 'Vanessa Smith called me at lunchtime and told me she heard a gunshot from the back of the farm. She said she saw Arthur driving back past the house and looked to be in a terrible mood from what she saw, so we can assume it has something to do with him and Tom.'

'Gunshot or gunshots?' He asked, knowing the difference mattered a whole lot in the current situation.

'One gunshot. Why, what are you thinking?'

'Could be a lot of things. Could be Tom shooting Roo's, we just don't know. But let's not take any chances.'

As they neared the rear of the property, Nick slowed the vehicle down now to walking pace. It looked quiet up ahead, with only Tom's old work ute parked under a large gum tree beside the property. 'Well, it's gone either one of two ways. Tom Smith has killed himself in there. Or Arthur Smith has confronted him and shot him.

'Let's hope it's not either of them.'

They approached the trailer with caution, and he parked behind the dense trees which surrounded the building. Slowly exiting the car, he pointed behind him at Maz to follow him, and put one finger up to his mouth for quiet. They held their weapons at the ready, both pointed towards the ground as they crept slowly towards the building. It was deathly quiet, the only sound being the birds in the trees and the slight breeze. He tried to use his senses to pick up any disturbances, whether there was anyone watching them or if they were in any danger. He felt none, but he knew that didn't mean there weren't any.

Maz worked her way slowly in front of him as they made the steps of Tom Smith's deck. She tiptoed up the old timber steps, and he followed with caution. The door to the trailer was wide open, and she got to the entrance and waited for him to reach her. 'What do you think?' she whispered to him.

'I think we're alone. He's done a runner, I reckon.'

A moment later, he heard a guttural groan come from inside the trailer. Maz's eyebrows raised, and he took the lead and walked inside the trailer. As he walked into the small entrance, he could see that it had been completely trashed. Drawers were flipped upside down, and a window was smashed, spreading glass all over the kitchen floor. Further onwards, he saw the back of a person's head and he held his gun up towards it.

'Tom? This is the police. Show me your hands.'

The figure remained still, and he slowly walked forward. All of his instincts screamed at him that something felt wrong. The figure began to cough, spluttering and wet, as he walked around the couch, to stare Tom Smith in the eyes.

Tom sat slouched on the old leather couch, with a gunshot wound to his heart. An old vintage pistol was to the left of him, and beside that, a glass pipe. His chest was an absolute mess, with blood flowing freely from just above his left hand-side chest pocket of his shirt. His knee had also been sliced open with a deep wound and it had a bloody dishcloth wrapped around it. The blood had flown down his leg and had begun to fill up his work boot. His face was red and purple with a fresh black eye that had begun to close up, and his nose looked to be broken. Whoever had done this to him hadn't wanted him to leave this trailer.

Tom's hand moved ever so slightly towards the pistol. 'Do not touch that gun,' Nick said. 'I swear to god, I'll put a bullet in you.'

Tom smiled a lopsided grin. With a missing front tooth, he coughed blood out of his mouth, and it dribbled down his chin. 'I'm dead already.'

Maz came up beside Nick and looked to be in shock. 'Who did this to you, Tom?'

Tom looked over at her with his broken smile. 'It doesn't matter.' He took one more ragged breath in, and with a great amount of effort said, 'Tell Art and Ness, I'm sorry.'

As the words came out of his mouth, his head tipped slowly forward, and Nick could tell he was gone. A small trickle of blood ran off his chin into his lap and the only sound in the old trailer was a game show on the TV behind them. He walked over and felt underneath his chin for a pulse and felt nothing. 'He's gone.'

Nick turned and sat down on the stool beside the dining table, with Maz following and doing the same. She looked like she'd aged ten years in the last week and Nick could tell it was taking a toll on her.

'What the hell is going on?' she asked.

'I don't know. But I think Arthur Smith has some explaining to do.'

Maz ran her fingers through her hair and grabbed a cigarette from her pocket, lighting it quickly before Nick could protest. 'I need this.'

He offered no resistance and let her sit in silence for a few minutes as he stared at Tom's body sitting on the old weathered couch. A glass pipe lay beside him with a lighter, and from what he could see on one of his arms were the deep scratches and scabs of a prominent user. It wasn't something he had noticed during any of their meetings and wondered just how he had hidden that so well from them. If he was a heavy drug user, he was surprised that the police didn't know about it. And wondered what connection that could have with Harry's murder and Belle's disappearance.

'Why would he want to tell Art and Ness that he's sorry?' he asked.

Maz took another drag of her cigarette and mulled it over. 'Guilt, I assume. Maybe it has something to do with Belle's disappearance?'

Nick sighed. 'Well, I guess we'll never know.'

Maz moved out onto the front deck of the trailer and had her second cigarette while Nick made phone calls. He spoke with Pat and Sam and told them to head to the homestead to see Vanessa and Bec, and to keep an eye out for Arthur. He then called Bec and updated her on what had happened.

'Shit Nick, what is happening?'

'I don't know. We won't know any more until you guys get on the scene, don't say anything to Vanessa for now. I don't know how much she knows. Let Sam and Pat talk to her.'

'Okay, I'll call Neville and get him to load up. We'll be there shortly.'

Chapter Thirty-Two

A small army had descended onto Tom's trailer by nightfall and Nick once again prepared for a long night. He felt like he had hardly stopped since the minute he had driven into town. Bec and Neville had busied themselves inside looking around and an ambulance from Mildura with a coroner was parked out front, waiting to retrieve Tom's body.

'No sign of Arthur Smith. Vanessa has been calling him all afternoon, nothing,' Pat said to Nick.

'Put out an alert for his registration. Hopefully, somebody sees his vehicle and gets onto us. Also, get an alert put on his bank cards and phone. He uses them anywhere and we'll ping him.'

'On it.'

He turned to Maz, who was sitting in one of the chairs up on the old deck with another cigarette in her hand. 'C'mon, let's have a look around.'

She put the cigarette out in the worn crystal ashtray sitting on the camping table and sighed. 'Good idea.'

Maz took the kitchen and made her way slowly through the drawers. As he searched through the small bedroom, he noticed something gleaming sticking out from the side of the bed. He got down on his hands and knees and reached down, and pulled out a pristine, well maintained .308 hunting rifle with a scope. He felt sure now his hunch had been right all along. Tom had shot Harry McKenzie. He passed the rifle off to Neville, who would submit it for testing that night, and he hoped that he was right.

After thoroughly searching the rest of the trailer, the two officers made their way outside to search around the property. Nick held his Maglite torch out in front of him as he walked towards the back of the trailer, illuminating a small path in front of the pair. Unlike the front, the rear had no decking or protection around it, and you could see the rusted axles and flat tyres sitting forlornly under the sagging weight of the old camper.

Nick spotted a small newer looking corrugated iron shed attached to the back corner of the trailer, with the doorway facing back towards them. He shone his torch over the small building. It was your average style garden shed, usually purchased at a hardware store, pine green in colour, and was hidden well behind the back of the trailer. 'This looks like a recent addition.'

Maz took the lead and walked over to the small shed. The door was firmly closed, and a large numerical padlock was affixed to the front latch. 'Give us a sec.,' she said, as she walked back off towards the front of the building.

While he waited, he walked around the small building and noticed piles of spoil heaped up along the fence line around a metre from the back of the building. It looked like someone had been doing some digging a while ago, he thought, as the piles were now smoothed off from years of rainfall. The hole must have been substantial, as it was built up to the height of the back barbed wire fence.

Maz returned a short time later with a pair of shiny new red bolt cutters. 'In Pat's car,' she replied to Nick's curious gaze. 'You never know when they might come in handy out here.'

She made quick work of the new lock and, with a satisfying click of the bolt cutters, swung the shed door inwards. 'After you.'

He made his way into the small shed and shone his flashlight around the small space; it was in a lot neater condition than the rest of the property; the floor was freshly swept and there wasn't a cobweb in sight. Two rows of shelving lined each wall and tools were hung from hooks on each side, with neat pattern outlines printed behind each one. Maz made her way in behind him and found a light switch beside the door. Warm light illuminated the small space, and they got to work slowly, looking through the toolbox and crates underneath the benches. After a few minutes, Maz got up off her knees and looked at Nick. He was kneeling in the centre of the shed, running his hands over the flooring.

'What is it?'

The shed floor was smooth concrete, but from the back rear bench and out towards the centre of the shed, a steel checker plate section of steel was recessed into the slab. There was a large rubber matt that was rolled up to the side, which look like it was used to hide the plate. He got up and walked over to the big red toolbox covered in stickers and pulled out a flat-bladed screwdriver.

'Did you see the dirt outside? I think there's something underground. I think it's a door.'

He tried to slide the blade into the millimetre thin gap between the steel plate and concrete slab and cursed as his hand slipped and knocked his knuckles on the plate, just as his hand hit it, he noticed the plate depress slightly and he looked back at Maz with a grin.

Placing both palms on the plate, he pressed downwards and felt a satisfying click, with the heavy trap door slowly rising in front of them. He now realised it was on an intricate air strut system that held it firmly in place. Shining his torch light down into the hole, he found a recessed cavity underneath the shed, one metre deep by two metres wide, lined with rubber matting at the base of it.

He smiled up at Maz. 'Well, whoever built this had something to hide.'

At the centre of the hole was a small, old wooden box. It looked like an old wooden packing crate cut in half, with a makeshift lid fixed firmly on the top of it. Next to it was a black sports bag. He held the torchlight firm while Maz reached down into the small chamber and pulled the box and bag out.

'Be very careful. Who knows what's in there? It could be dangerous.'

Maz sat the bag up on the bench first and unzipped it slowly. They both peeked inside, and his suspicions were now confirmed. The bag was full of thousands of dollars' worth of drugs. Small packets were taped neatly together and stacked with precision. This was a commercial quantity; Tom had been dealing.

'I knew it. I knew he was still involved in it somehow. What's in the box?'

Maz shook the box ever so gently, and they heard something rustle inside. 'Feels pretty empty, maybe some papers?'

She placed it gently onto the bench top and Nick clicked his torch off. They stood underneath the singular light globe in the shed and he cautiously opened the lid. There were three old manilla envelopes inside and he pulled them out separately. He passed one over to Maz and opened one for himself. They were full of old Polaroid pictures and some newer style disposable camera images.

'Oh my god,' Maz said as she held her hands up over her mouth.

Nick looked through the old photos of Belle and Anna at a lake, in various stages of undress, some were in swimmers and some were a lot worse, and looked like when they were asleep. He felt sick to his stomach with some of the things he was seeing and felt rage boiling up inside him. He slid each photo back inside the manilla envelope and made his way back out of the shed into the cool night air. He looked up at the stars for a minute, lost in thought, and waited for Maz to join him.

'Well, I think we can guess what happened to Belle Smith.'

'Can we?' she asked.

He nodded. 'I think Tom was sexually abusing her. What if it all came to a head out at the lake and she confronted him?'

'Maybe.'

'I don't think we'll ever truly have an answer,' he said. 'But it's enough for me.'

The next afternoon Nick and Maz sat together in the Police station, quietly sipping takeaway cups of coffee bought from the local café. He had got back to the pub at around 3am after everyone had finished for the night and had managed five hours of restless sleep while Bailey snored on the end of the bed.

Pat came through the entranceway of the office and made his way over to Maz and Nick with a tired smile. 'Preliminary results are back from the rifle we found underneath Tom Smith's bed.'

'And?' he asked.

'It's a match. That's the gun that killed McKenzie.'

He was right all along; he thought to himself, but it still didn't explain why he did it. What motive did Tom Smith have to kill Harry McKenzie?

'I knew it. I had a bad feeling about him from the start.'

'God, you were right. I still just don't understand why,' Maz replied.

Nick and Maz had both mutually agreed to keep the photos they had found in the shed quiet for now. They didn't want word to get around about them, especially with Anna still living in the town. They needed to speak with Vanessa and Arthur before any further decisions were made.

'I think Harry confronted Tom and accused him of having something to do with Belle's disappearance,' he said.

'It still doesn't explain how her school uniform got on Harry's farm,' Maz said.

Nick sipped from his coffee, lost in thought. Most of the pieces were coming together, but he felt like something was amiss. What was he missing? He felt like there was more to it. Harry McKenzie had lived next door to the Smiths' forever. Why did Tom take all this time to kill him? If he was such a threat, he could've done it years ago.

Moments later, Rita popped her head around the corner and yelled out in their direction, 'You can cancel the search for Arthur Smith. He and Vanessa just parked out the front.'

They both stood from their seats and made their way to the entrance of the station. Maz put her arm on Nick's elbow gently, and he realised he had his hand sitting on the top of his service weapon at the ready. 'I don't think you'll be needing that, Detective,' Maz said to him.

Vanessa had her arm wrapped around Arthur's shoulders and he looked like he was crying from where they stood. His usual stoop was even more pronounced, and his eyes were fixed directly toward the footpath as they walked in through the entrance doors.

'Hi Maz, we'd like to have a word with you two if possible?' Vanessa asked.

'Of course, come through, please.'

The four sat in the cramped interview room, which doubled as a storage room in the back of the station. The back wall was lined with office supplies and storage boxes, all lined with a thick layer of dust. Nick was sure it was the first time someone had been in the room for a few years.

He looked at Arthur and Vanessa. They both looked like they had been through the wringer. Vanessa's cheeks were red, and her eyes were swollen and puffy. Arthur didn't look much better, and he, too, looked like he had been crying.

Nick placed his notepad down on the table along with his iPhone, setting it to record. He wasn't sure what direction their chat would go, but thought it would be good to keep a record of it.

'So, start from the beginning, please,' he said to Arthur.

Arthur wiped his nose with his sleeve and took a long deep breath in and began. 'Ever since I got back to Darfield, I've protected him. Yes, I have a past like everyone, but I went straight. I left it all behind to start a new life. And we have been happy here, we were happy here. Until we lost Belle, at least.'

'I assume we are talking about your brother?' he asked.

Arthur nodded. 'He was in with a bad crowd when we were growing up and he was caught dealing. I knew by moving out here I'd get him away from it all, but it followed us. He started using years ago, and I tried my best to mask it from the family. He was unpredictable, but in the end, he listened to me. And I knew I could protect him if he stayed on the farm.' His voice began to crack, and his bottom lip quivered. 'I just can't believe he's gone.'

Nick knew that he had to tell them about the photos, but wanted to push Arthur a little harder before he went there. 'Tell me about the drugs, Arthur.'

Arthur had rehearsed this conversation in his head already and knew now with Tom gone that he could conveniently palm all the blame off on his dead stepbrother. It would offer another fresh start for him and Vanessa. And if the dealers ever turned back up, he would have to worry about that problem when it arose.

'It started small. One of Tom's old friends came to visit us years ago. He loved it out on the farm. The remoteness of it all, and he realised he could use it to his advantage. Darfield is nearly centre to Sydney, Melbourne, and Adelaide and the farm was a convenient location to store product.'

That explained the elaborate bunker setup in the rear shed. He wasn't sure just how big the operation was, but going across various state lines seemed big enough. 'And did he sell the product himself?' Nick asked.

'God no. Not at first. All he did was get a call from time to time and a truck would turn up. He would pack it in the hole, leave it for a month or two, and someone would come past and pick it up. That was it.'

Vanessa cut in. 'Technically, Art wasn't even breaking any laws.'

'He had ownership of illegal substances on their property. That is breaking the law, Vanessa,' he replied.

'And how did you know all this? How were you involved?' he asked Arthur.

'He broke down to me a few years ago. I told him I didn't want anything to do with it, and to get that shit off our farm. He didn't listen to me.'

Nick continued, 'You said he wasn't dealing at first? Did he start to sell?'

'Yes, I think so. I think that's how we got here. His using really started after Belle disappeared. I don't know what switch flipped inside of him, but he changed. He got angry and dark. Sometimes he wouldn't leave his trailer for weeks. I would just do his share on the farm and hide it as best I could. The whole town never liked us from the minute we moved here. If they heard my brother was a druggie, how would that of went?'

Nick noted that Arthur said the big change was when Belle disappeared. Tom Smith was guilty about something more, that was for sure.

Arthur sighed. 'In the last year, he had started to pull back from me even more, and I could tell he was using again.'

'So what happened in the trailer?' Maz asked.

'The repercussions of his actions, that's what. The suppliers came to pick up their product, and it was all gone. Tom had been selling it from under our noses. As you saw, they weren't happy.'

Tom's face had been beaten to a pulp and now they understood why. The gangs that ruled the drug trade, especially ones big enough to cross interstate lines, were vicious. And wouldn't have taken the news that their product was being sold under their noses lightly.

'They beat the shit out of him. I got there before it was too late and ran them off, but you saw what they did to him.'

'So why did you run then?' Maz asked.

Arthur sighed and looked down at the floor. 'I was scared, I guess. I knew if you found him, you would've thought it was me. I was so angry after you told me about the camping trip, and I wanted to confront him.'

Telling them about the camping trip felt like a week ago in Nick's mind, when it was barely 24 hours earlier. He knew Arthur had been angry, and he wondered if he got the chance to ask his brother about it. Before he could ask, Arthur continued, 'And you lot were wrong. I asked him about it, and nothing happened. I knew you lot had it wrong.'

Nick looked across at Maz and knew that he had to be the one to break the news to them. It wasn't going to be pretty, but he knew what he had to do. 'There's something else you both need to know.'

'What?' Vanessa asked.

He got up and walked back out towards Maz's desk and reached into the top drawer. Together, on their way back into town, they separated the photos they had come across and put the worst of the worst in one folder, the moderate in another and the tamest in the last. He grabbed the tamest of the three out and made his way back into the small room. 'We found these in the back shed behind Tom's trailer,' he explained, as he opened the old folder and fanned various photo's out on the table.

Vanessa gasped and placed both of her shaking hands over her mouth when she realised what she was seeing. Arthur's expression was blank, and his hand slowly picked a photo up of his missing daughter and he looked at it closely. 'What the fuck is this?' he asked.

'There were hundreds of images we found in a small box in his shed. Some are a lot worse than this, to be honest, and we won't be showing you those. We are both really sorry.'

He let the information wash over them as Vanessa started to cry quietly, and continued, 'I think it's safe for us to assume that Belle confronted Tom on this camping trip. Maybe she knew about the photos or found them? Or maybe she told him she was going to tell you both about them. We believe that after this altercation, Tom used the fires as a diversion and killed Belle and disposed of her body.'

They both continued to look at the photos in silence. Nick knew that it would've been hard to take it all in and would come as a shock to them that someone in their own family was capable of what they were seeing.

'I, I don't believe it,' Arthur finally said after what felt like five minutes. 'He was my brother. Why would he do this?'

'People are complex, Arthur; he was a sick man. He would've lived a life of shame after knowing what he did to you both. We think that's why he committed suicide,' Maz replied.

'What?'

Arthur's face had a mixture of shock and sadness in his eyes. 'What do you mean, he committed suicide?'

Nick opened the coroner's preliminary report and read out loud, 'Multiple broken facial bones, nose, cheekbone and eye socket, knife laceration in knee hitting the femoral artery and finally, a single gunshot wound entering the right side of the heart causing massive blood loss.'

He looked up at the couple. 'We got to him just as he was dying. His last words were, tell Art and Ness that I am sorry.'

Chapter Thirty-Three

Nick sat at his dining table in his home in Sydney. He had paperwork spread from one side of the table to the other, with a mixture of the original case files Maz had given him, his own written reports, and paperwork he had photocopied from Harry McKenzie's home office.

Rain lashed at his windows and a particularly bad storm was due to come across the city that night. Just as he looked out at the dark clouds, his lights flickered ever so slightly, and he shivered in the gloom. He felt like the minute he left Darfield the weather had been grey, and he hadn't seen the sun since his last days there.

He looked over into the kitchen and watched Bec as she made coffee on his machine. It was a gift from his sister, and he still hadn't quite figured out how to use it, but he watched as she expertly let the machine steam and hiss, and the smell of perfectly brewed coffee soon began to fill the room. She wore one of his work shirts, and her long brown legs were crossed as she stood, deep in concentration.

He had to smile as he looked at her. The minute the case wrapped up, she decided to take leave and had spent her last four weeks in Sydney, spending time with Nick and catching up with friends. He felt an ease with her he hadn't felt with anyone else in a long time. Different women had come and gone but not someone who intimately knew how he worked, and he thought maybe, just maybe, he could start to see a long-term future with her.

The last four weeks had been a blur, and he felt drained after the day he had had. His Chief had asked him on his day off to come in and meet with a senior media liaison to discuss his time in Darfield. As she sat and spoke with him, and he ran through the same lines he had written in his report which had been read and discussed by most people in this office by now, his mind trailed away, and he could still feel something at the back of his mind nagging at him.

It seemed to be all tied up, neatly in a bow for everyone except him, and he still felt like something was missing. Yes, Tom Smith killed Harry McKenzie, and yes, he had taken advantage of Belle, but there was one thing he and Maz could not get to the bottom of. How had he killed her, and where was the body? The hardest thing for him now was knowing that he would probably never have an answer, and what they had discovered was enough to close it, and enough for Arthur and Vanessa.

Arthur hadn't taken the news well, and it took him some time to believe his brother was capable of it. Vanessa was a different story. As soon as Maz and he had explained everything they had found, it was like a switch was flipped inside her and a load was taken off her shoulders. She believed that Tom did it, and she told them deep down that maybe she had known all along.

Bec padded back from the kitchen into the dining area and placed a coffee down in front of him. She sat in the chair across from him and placed one smooth leg on his lap with a smile. 'Foot rub?'

He reached down and wrapped his hand around her foot and slowly squeezed it, kneading his thumbs up and along her main bone connected to her big toe.

'Mmm, that's good. My feet are killing me. Annie made me walk all the way to Bondi.'

Nick had done the same walk Bec had made many times, a picturesque walk along the ocean side. He wished he could've been there with her today, and not doing what he had to do.

'Are you ok?'

He sighed. 'Yeah, long day.'

She slid the closest piece of paper on the table towards herself, a colour school photograph of Belle, one of the last photos taken of her. 'You're not going to let this go, are you?'

'I'm going to have to. Life goes on. The Smiths have the answers they were looking for.'

'But do you?'

'No. I don't.'

The next morning, he had woken up early before Bec and snuck out for a morning run. The storm that the news had built up for more than a week had gone off without a whimper and the morning sky was clear, with warm rays of sunshine beginning to break across the horizon. He looked down at his watch as he slowed near his driveway and paused his workout; he was surprised at his time, almost 30 seconds quicker than the last time he had run that route even though he hardly remembered running it. His mind was still in Darfield.

Walking back through his front door, the house was still silent, and he made his way quietly back into his bedroom to have a quick shower. Bec stirred and rolled over towards him with a smile. 'Morning.'

He still found it hard to believe a woman as beautiful as her could be in his bed with such little clothing and did his to best to suppress a grin. 'Good morning to you too.'

'How was your run?'

'Easier than I thought it would be. Hey, listen, I know it's Sunday, but I've got to run into the office. The Chief wants to see me.'

She smiled. 'Hey remember, I'm the one on holiday. You do what you need to do. I'll be here.'

He quickly showered and put on his usual head office attire and made his way in. It was shaping up to be a beautiful Sunday and he would've rather spent it out with Bec, but he knew when the Chief wanted to see him in person that it would be important.

Making his way through the top level, he wasn't surprised to see it humming with activity, but was surprised to see a couple of the senior inspectors at their desks. Unusual for a Sunday, he thought. The clear glass walls of the Chief's office offered no privacy and he could see that another person was sitting in front of his desk, deep in conversation.

He knocked lightly on the glass door and the Chief motioned for him to come in. 'Nick, sorry to bring you in on a Sunday, mate. How are you?'

'Morning. What's this all about?'

Sitting across from the Chief was a young woman, in her mid to late twenties. She had short, dark hair and wore a tight black pencil skirt, with a similar shade blouse. The main thing that caught his eye, however, was her black and grey sleeve tattoo, which ran from the top of her shoulder and completely covered her left hand.

'This is Hattie. She's an IT analyst for us here, missing persons.'

Nick reached across to shake her hand and smile. 'Nick Vada, pleasure to meet you.'

She returned his smile. 'Your reputation proceeds you detective.' She turned back towards the Chief and spoke in a thick European accent. 'As I was saying, I wanted you to hear it first. It is weird yes? I know it could be nothing, but it's something we should check out?' The Chief leant back in his chair and rubbed the stubble on his chin, lost in thought.

'What is it?' Nick asked.

'Brittany Reardon,' Hattie answered.

Nick hadn't heard the name since his time back in Darfield. The name on Belle's fake ID.

'What about it? We ran the name through the database as soon as we heard about it.'

Hattie smirked. 'Your database is a bit more antiquated than what I use.'

'So what are you saying exactly?'

'It is standard procedure on high-profile cases for our specialised analyst team to undertake further searches with our latest systems. We noticed one of the Darfield officers searching for hits on the driver's licence and come back with nothing. I myself took a shine to this case from listening to the podcast and thought I would do some more investigation.'

'And what did you find?'

'We searched all social media platforms, insurance records, hospital and medical records, local and state newspapers, and now we also use facial recognition and AI voice monitoring on devices.'

Nick felt like she was playing with him now and was starting to feel the frustration of his wasted Sunday building up. He butt in. 'This all could've been explained over an email or call.'

'Let her finish,' The Chief replied.

Nick sighed. 'I'm sorry, it's been a long few weeks.'

'It's ok. As I was saying. We tried all of those things, and we did find a few peculiarities. We found a Brittany Rearden with an e instead of an o, the same age as Belle Smith, who transferred from a NSW driver's licence to a NT licence in Alice Springs, May 2002. Yearly renewal has been paid ever since, also an ANZ bank account which was opened using that same new ID.'

'So different spelling to what we had?'

'Only slightly, our systems have the capacity to run through millions of combinations, and spelling differences are one of them.'

'Look, it's a longshot. It's still only a single driver's licence and a bank account. What's saying there isn't another Brittany Rearden who was born in Alice Springs who just got her driver's licence?'

'Using that different spelling, we searched every known database and social media account that our computers could manage, and it only turned up that driver's licence and bank account.'

'Why do I get the feeling you're not telling me something?'

The Chief smiled and passed a piece of paper over the desk to him. It was an older document that looked like it had been photocopied multiple times and possibly sent by fax. It was dated 1st of May 2005.

To Whom It May Concern,

Please see attached copy of a Ms Brittany Rearden's NSW Driver's Licence. This licence was used as a state transfer into our system. After further assessment from our team, we believe it may be a part of the counterfeit batch that you have been having issues with. We have tried to contact Miss Rearden but have had no answer. Please submit for further testing and we will await your reply.

NT, Department of Transport.

Nick held the piece of paper in his hands and quickly noticed that they were shaking. Surely, after all of this, how could he be so wrong?

Hattie noticed the look of shock on his face and continued. 'Our system found this buried deep in an archive folder when we searched for the different spelling. It looks like Belle or someone else used the fake ID to transfer into a real driver's licence. As far as I've found so far, nothing was ever done after this document was sent.

Nick just stared blankly at Hattie and felt like his last two months had been turned upside down. Everything that everyone had told him was either wrong or a lie. 'So you're telling me Belle Smith, the most famous face in the nation, walked into a Department of Transport building in 2005 and changed her licence over, and all we have is this single document? It was five years after she went missing. Why did she wait so long?'

Hattie shrugged. 'That I can't tell you. I assume she was waiting until she thought it was safe to try?'

Nick thought it was flimsy, but it was a fresh lead and he knew thought that maybe there could be something more to it. 'Ok, so I guess I'll make a few calls, and see what I can find out,' he said.

'Also, we have a current address,' Hattie said.

The Chief leaned forward in his chair, and the decision was made. 'Nick, you need to go there. You need to try. I think she's still alive. Go and find her.'

Chapter Thirty-Four

Nick sat facing the tarmac and felt the sun blazing through the high glass windows. He'd never been to the Mildura Airport before but looking around, it felt like any of the small regional airports he had been to. It had a solitary café, which sold overpriced coffee and days old sandwiches, and a small gift shop which doubled as a newsagent and bookshop.

He watched as the small twin-engine plane descended from the clouds, starting from a speck on the horizon. The landing gear came down as the plane was nearing the tarmac and it made a smooth landing, and slowly taxied to a stop.

The last twenty-four hours had been a whirlwind on top of the last two months he had had, and the minute he left the police headquarters, the first thing he did was find a quiet coffee shop to call Maz Rogers. She was similarly blown away like Nick and couldn't believe that, after all this time that Belle Smith may be still alive. After going over fully what they had found and sending it through email straight to her, he agreed to fly straight to Mildura and pick her up on the way through to Alice Springs.

He watched as Maz made her way over with two tall takeaway coffee cups. Steam emanated from both of them and he knew that taking a sip right now would be lethal.

'I asked for extra hot. They let us take these on the plane,' Maz said.

'Good thinking, I much prefer this airport security to the cities. How's Bailey?'

'She's good, her beds under the bar, so she spends a lot of her days with Dan now. It's nice and warm beside the fridge motors, so no complaints from her.'

'Good to hear.' He was happy she had found a safe home.

They both sat with their small bags and watched as passengers disembarked from the tiny plane as the ground crew fuelled it up. 'So what's the plan?' Maz asked.

Nick had been pouring over the finer details of everything that Hattie had found on his flight over and did some further research himself. Even with everything he had, it still felt light on detail. 'We hire a car. And start at that address. It's as good a plan as we are going to get.'

Maz sipped her coffee and looked out the window. 'I just can't believe all of this. Surely she couldn't be alive?'

'Let's not get too excited. Like I said to the Chief, it could be a coincidence. How have Arthur and Vanessa been?'

'I haven't spoken to them this week, but I popped in last Friday and they were ok. Joe was there for the weekend, so we caught up. Arthur has taken Tom's death hard. Even after everything that happened.'

Nick couldn't understand how Arthur could grieve Tom after what he had done. The photos he saw were some of the worst things he had seen in his policing career, and he had seen a lot of things.

'What did you do with the photos?'

'I submitted them as evidence into the Smith file.'

He lifted the lid on his coffee cup and blew softly at the boiling milk. 'I'm glad you did. Who knows what's going to happen here?'

After another half an hour of fuelling, they soon boarded and made the short plane ride to Alice Springs. Maz sat engrossed in the thin folder which held the various pieces of paperwork that Hattie had managed to uncover during her search. The plane was small, much smaller than Nick was comfortable on, but he knew that this might be the most important plane ride of his entire life and tried to look out the small window at the barren land below, and try not to think about them hitting the ground. When they landed, they were both smacked in the face by the hot, dry heat of the outback. They were both used to heat, but this was a different level up here.

'Jesus Christ, it's hot,' Maz said, as she used the document holder to swat away the flies covering her face.

Nick's phone started to ping as he descended the small aluminium staircase. One unread message had popped up from Bec.

'Hope your flight was okay. Good luck xx.'

When he had got home from his visit to the Chief, he had laid out the entire sequence of events. Bec sat and listened intently and smiled when he come to his conclusion. She wished him luck and told him she was heading home to get back to work herself.

He was slightly disappointed that she was leaving, but knew after a few weeks that she would have had to return to Mildura soon, anyway; he felt like there were words left unsaid, but he knew he had unfinished business with this case, and couldn't focus on his personal life right now. It would have to wait, and he knew she understood. That's what he loved about her.

Not taking any checked in bags saved them from going through the luggage area at the airport, and they quickly made their way through toward the hire cars. The counters were all empty and, after calling the number on the bench-top, an exasperated man came running through the doors to the counter.

'Hi, I pre-booked a Landcruiser, Nick Vada?'

The man wiped the sweat from his brow and quickly busied himself with the keyboard. 'Yes, one Toyota Landcruiser. I have one out in the lot ready for you now, Mr. Vada, just the two days?'

'For now, thanks.'

After signing all the documentation and handing over his identification, they were soon on the road and heading for the main highway. Nick looked up his maps on his phone and typed in the address. It was 550km's from Alice Springs. He placed his phone up on the dashboard as Maz drove, and she looked beside the steering wheel at the distance on it.

'Far out. You never get used to just big it is out here. What's the name of the place again?'

'Tranbie Station,' Nick said, from the research he had made the night previous. 'The 11th biggest station in the Northern Territory, run by the Cannon family, mostly cattle and goat farming. The closest fuel and shop is Barrow Creek, 150kms away.'

'Now I know why we got this car.'

'Yep, long range tank, you need it out here.'

'So what's the plan of attack? We just going to show up and ask if they've heard of a Brittany Rearden?'

'Have you got a better idea? I didn't want to phone or anything. I'd rather have the element of surprise here. Who knows what they could be hiding?'

'Fair enough.'

The road was long and gun barrel straight beyond the car, and felt like it could go on forever. He looked out the window at the shimmering road in the heat and now, being here, understood that a person could probably come out here and never be found. He wanted badly to find out what had happened to Belle, but knew that their search would probably be futile, a wild goose chase. What were the odds that she would still be at this address, 23 years later? It was a long shot, but he knew he could never rest until he had the answer.

The minutes stretched into hours and they had switched places after Maz told Nick she was tiring. Looking in the distance, he noticed some buildings, and realised they must be nearing Barrow Creek. As they got to the roadhouse, he found it was more a row of different sized sheds, all in various states of disrepair. A large metal structure had been built over the pumps to protect them from the sun and rain, and it looked to be the only thing built in this century.

Maz busied herself with fuelling up, and he got out and reached his arms over his head for a stretch. They were the only car at the station, and he noticed two young boys sitting at a picnic table under the shade of the trees, watching him warily. He gave a small wave and looked out across the vast expanse. What a childhood. Surely, you'd die of boredom, he thought to himself quietly.

'You want anything from inside?' he asked Maz.

'A Diet Coke, and a pack of Marlboro Reds.'

'I thought you were giving them up?'

She chuckled. 'You said that, not me.'

He walked under the shade of the pump roof and felt relief from the relentless sun. The old structure cracked and ticked in the severe heat, and he wondered how people could live here day in and day out. He soon answered his own question as he walked through the automatic doors into the building. The air conditioning was blasting, and it felt like he needed to put a jacket on. It was freezing inside the small building. An older woman sat at the register and offered a smile in his direction. 'How are you darlin'?'

'I'm well, thank you,' he replied, as he grabbed some drinks from the fridges and made his way over to the counter. 'Just this and the fuel, please.'

She brought up the total on the machine. 'That'll be $215.60 please.'

'Shit, sorry, also a pack of Marlboro Red's please.'

She glanced at him from over her glasses. 'Terrible habit. You sure you need them?'

'There for my partner.'

'Fair enough.'

He tapped his work card on the machine on the counter and began to make his way to the door and had a thought, turning back towards the attendant he opened his wallet and displayed his police ID. 'I'm Detective Nick Vada, from the NSW police force, would you mind if I asked you a couple of questions?'

The attendant looked at him for a beat and then cracked a big smile. 'Oooo police, how exciting, I'll have to tell my husband you were in. Yes, of course, what is it?'

A boring life out here, Nick thought. At least she seemed to offer no resistance. 'Trambie Station, you ever have anyone in there from here?'

She looked almost disappointed. 'Oh, I thought you were going to hit me with something interesting. Yeah, we get workers from time to time. The Cannons were here last week actually, now I remember. On their way back from holidays I think Alex said, went to the Gold Coast.'

'Does the name Brittany Rearden ring any bells to you?' he asked.

She offered a blank expression. 'Rearden.. Rearden. No nothing, I'm sorry.'

'It's okay,' he replied as he passed his card over the counter. 'If you ever hear that name out here, give me a call.'

'Alex's wife's name is Brittany, if that helps? I'm not sure her maiden name, though.'

Nick stopped dead in his tracks. He opened his phone and scrolled through his photos to one of the last photos he had of Belle.

'Does she look anything like this?' he said, as he handed the phone over to her.

The elderly lady pushed her glasses up and leaned over the counter. 'Hmmm, hard to say, my eyesight isn't what it used to be. It certainly could be, though. She sort of looks similar.'

Nick was slightly disappointed, but knew that it was more than a massive coincidence. Could Belle be still alive? And on Tranbie station?

The last 150kms went quicker than he thought they would as the sun began to descend toward the horizon. Nick filled Maz in on what the petrol station owner had said, and although it seemed like they were on the right track, he struggled to understand how Belle could have made it this far without being recognised all this time. They both agreed that if it was a dead end, they would turn back and take turns driving back to Alice Springs, it was going to be a long day and even longer night, but if it meant they could find some answers, they were willing to put in the work.

The small blue dot on his maps app soon showed that they were nearing their destination, and they both looked out across the vast expanse. There was nothing but red dirt, shrubs, and a straight fence line on their right of the highway, as far as the eye could see, and Nick wondered why you would ever want to farm in this region.

He soon slowed the car down when he noticed a gate and a lone tree shading some signage. The sign under the tree read 'Welcome to Tranbie' in neat paintwork. The sign looked quite new, he noted and glistened in the fading sunlight. Beside it were two large galvanised metal gates that stood open, and he crawled slowly over the cattle grates which sat between them.

'Looks like we're here.'

A long dirt driveway led out from the gates into the horizon, and from what he could see, there were no close signs of civilization. He sped up to a comfortable pace and settled in for the drive to the homestead. Looking down at his odometer, he realised they had travelled ten kilometres already, when he began to see signs of buildings in the distance. Neat fencing lined each side of the driveway, and every few kilometres they passed intersections of fencing that formed huge cattle pens. As they got closer to the homestead, they noticed the hundreds of cattle lining each pen, and they looked curiously at the hire car as it made the journey past.

The red dirt of the driveway soon turned into a light grey crushed rock and Nick swung his car into the entrance of the homestead. A palm tree stood in solitude in the front of the property and various farm vehicles were parked around it, in a rough circle that formed the driveway.

The homestead itself was huge, a long and low red brick building with a white corrugated iron roof. A windmill rose up from the far-left-hand side of the building and two huge black water tanks flanked the base of it. To the right of the homestead were two huge sheds, both with their doors closed. The property was well kept, and everything looked pristine.

'The Cannon family look well off,' Maz said.

'There's big money in livestock.'

Just as they got out of the car and both stretched, Nick heard the rumble of a motorbike. Soon, from around the back side of the homestead, the bike came into view and the man riding it pulled up metres away from them and came to a stop.

He was tall and wiry and had faded jeans with a neat button up work shirt. On top of his head was a well-worn Akubra hat. He looked to be around Nick's age, he guessed, and was well tanned from many years on the land in the sun. He swung his leg off the machine and walked over to them with an expression of curiosity. 'Help you?'

'How are you, mate? I'm Detective Sergeant Nick Vada and this is Sergeant Maz Rogers. We are with the NSW police force. Hoping we could ask you a few questions?'

He held out his hand and was relieved when the farmer took it, giving it a firm shake. 'Alex Cannon. Wow, you lot are a long way from home! Of course. How can I help?'

'Tell us about it,' Maz replied. 'We are actually looking for a missing person whose last known address was this property. Have you ever heard of a Brittany Rearden?'

His smile flickered ever so slightly at the name, Nick thought, and after a moment, he looked back at the house. 'I have. You guys hungry? Come inside.'

Nick looked over at Maz with his eyebrows raised and shrugged. Alex pulled the keys from the motorbike's ignition and walked towards the front entrance of the house as they followed. When he got there, he slid his boots off and placed them neatly on the rack beside the door. When Nick bent down to do the same, he waved them off. 'Don't you two stress unless you've been walking in cow shit like me.'

The house was just as clean inside as it was out, and they could both smell something delicious coming from the back of the house. He could hear music on in the background and small children running around inside. The floors were polished to a high shine, and old photos of the farm throughout the years flanked each side of the passageway.

When they got to the end of the hallway, they walked into an expansive living area and kitchen, which was a hive of activity. An elderly lady was standing in front of the stove stirring a pot, and two young boys wrestled on the couch. They both came to a stop when they walked into the room and Alex spoke in their direction. 'Boys, go wash up for dinner.'

They both nodded in unison while staring at Nick and Maz. Soon they had run off in the direction of what he assumed what their bathroom.

'Mum, where's Britt?'

The elderly woman looked at Nick and Maz in confusion. 'She's out hanging the washing, love. What's this about?'

Alex ignored his mother and continued on through towards the back-sliding door. 'Britt!'

'I'll be a minute, babe!' came a voice from outside.

Nick and Maz followed and made their way out onto the back deck. It looked like an oasis with rolling green grass rolling outwards into the harsh red desert. A clothesline was off to the left-hand side of the path and Nick could make out a shadow of a woman behind the white sheets, which were glowing in the sunset.

'Britt,' Alex said, pointing in her direction.

Maz elbowed her way past them both and jumped down off the back steps of the porch towards the woman. He walked slower and watched as Maz got to the clothesline before him. Just as she reached it, the wind blew the sheet across, and standing before him was Belle Smith.

Belle dropped the washing basket and put both of her hands up to her mouth.

'Belle?' Maz asked.

'Maz, what are you doing here?!'

Chapter Thirty-Five

Belle sat at the dinner table quietly, not speaking a word to anyone. The TV was on in the background and she could hear the news playing. 'Records continue to fall as we entered our third day over forty degrees, with no end in sight. Hospitalisations in the region have skyrocketed, with the elderly being admitted due to the scorching conditions. The region is bracing itself for high winds over the next week, which will raise the possibility of bushfires. We ask that the community follow their fire safety plans, and always stay prepared.'

Arthur grunted with a mouthful of mashed potato. 'We haven't had a bushfire in this region in years. There's nothing to burn. I don't know why they say stuff like that, just trying to scare everyone.'

Vanessa nodded and looked over towards Belle. 'You okay, love? You've barely touched your dinner.'

Belle looked down at her plate and played with a single pea with her fork. 'I'm not hungry. Can I go to bed?'

Vanessa sighed. 'Wait till your uncle Tom gets here and eats at least. It'd be rude not to wait for him.'

Belle felt her blood run cold and felt bile rising in her stomach. She had felt sick about their usual family Tuesday dinner night since the weekend, and dreaded seeing her uncle, but didn't want her Mum to know just yet what was going on. 'Okay,' she replied.

Just as she answered, she saw a dark figure sliding the back door open. Tom walked into the back of the house towards the dining area and smiled in their direction. She felt hot all over and closed her mouth in case she was sick.

'Evening all, shit, this looks good, Ness.'

He sat down and began to eat, talking with Arthur, Vanessa, and Joe while she sat and watched him. How could he come into their family home after what he did to her? She had awoken the morning after in her tent and had cried as the flashes of the night came back to her in fits and spurts. She was scared and confused. Why would he do that to her? And who could she tell? Anna would tell her parents if she said anything, and her Dad would kill him if she told him. She thought for a time about going to Maz Rogers; she was the nice lady police officer who was the Mum of one of her classmates at school but didn't know how to tell her. She felt so scared and so alone and wasn't sure what her next move would be.

After dinner, she quickly grabbed the dishes off the table and did her best to stay as far away from Tom as she possibly could. She could smell alcohol on his breath and gagged at it with memories of that night coming back to the forefront. She placed the dishes in the sink and looked over at her Mum. 'Mum, I'm not feeling well. I'm gonna head to bed.'

Vanessa nodded and said, 'Fair enough love, night.'

She sat in her room and fumed. How could he come into her house and pretend like that? She needed to do something, but she wasn't quite sure yet. After she had calmed down, she put her CD player on and tried to pretend he wasn't still in her house. Just as she was thinking about turning it off and going to bed, she heard heavy footsteps coming down the hallway. 'Night Joey, I'll just tell Belle goodnight and I'll be off Ness.'

She froze, and unable to think of what to do next, she pulled the covers high over her head as the door handle turned and she felt him walk into her room. 'I know you're still awake,' he said coldly.

She pulled the covers down over her face and looked at her uncle in the eyes. 'If you touch me, I will scream. Get the hell away from me. I'm going to tell Mum and Dad.'

He blinked coolly and looked back towards the door. 'If you say a word. To anyone, I'll fuckin kill ya. I'm deadly serious.' And with that turned on his heel and left the room.

The next week was a blur, and she turned in on herself completely. She ignored everybody, her family, her friends, and she started to hatch an idea of what she might do. When she heard the news of the bushfires approaching the region, she finally knew what she was going to do.

Before bed the night before, she packed a small backpack and dressed in dark jeans and a shirt. She stood in the centre of her bedroom and looked around, realizing it would be the last time she would ever stand in there again. She had said her goodbyes to her family in her own small way and knew that until her uncle was out of their life, she would never be truly safe here ever again.

Once nightfall came, she slipped out of her window and into the darkness, and made her way out into the backyard under the cover of the moon. She stood at her Dad's workbench in front of an old mirror resting against the back wall and, using scissors she'd stolen out of her brother's room, hacked her hair into a rough, shorter cut.

She did her best to pick up all the loose strands of her hair she had cut and put them in her backpack. She looked back at herself in the faded and cracked mirror. She still looked like her, but it was a start, and she pulled her hoodie over her head and made her way on foot out into the night, and said goodbye to her home, forever.

It had been easier than she thought, and she had only walked along the highway for a short while, when soon she heard the sound of a huge rumbling semi beginning to slow to a stop, she had grabbed a sharp screwdriver from her Dads workbench, and kept it up her jumper sleeve, just in case. Her senses were on such high alert after what had happened, and she felt like she knew now that she would have what it takes to survive. She just needed to be as far away from Darfield as possible.

The truck moved over into the table drain and slowed to a stop; it was huge, and she could see it was carting livestock, she could smell the cows, and could hear them loudly moving back and forwards in the huge trailer.

The passenger side window soon buzzed down, and she pulled her hoodie as low down over her face as she could. 'Hey, you ok?' the truckie said from his driver's seat.

She climbed up the metal steps and to the window opening. 'Hey, yeah I'm ok, my boyfriend and I had a fight, and he left me here.'

The truckie's brow furrowed. 'He left you? Far out, dangerous place to leave you. Where are you off to?'

She had read the writing on the door of the truck as she had climbed the steps. 'Woodford Livestock, Alice Springs.' And knew that was a long, long way from home. 'North, we're backpacking up towards Alice Springs,' she replied.

The cool night air was still between them, and she could tell that the truckie was deciding what to do. 'Shit, I'm on my way there too, best I can do is drop you at a roadhouse in town. You'll have to find your boyfriend from there, all right?'

She opened the door and climbed into the cabin. Sitting in the passenger seat, she did her best to keep her hoodie down, and was thankful it was dark inside. 'Thank you so much, I have a little money if you nee..'

The truckie waved her away. 'Don't be stupid. I'm not leaving you out here in the dark. The name's Scott, by the way. What's your name?'

It was going to take a while to get used to, she thought, but here goes nothing. 'Brittany.'

Chapter Thirty-Six

The sun had finally set across the vast horizon, and the temperature had dropped considerably from when they first stepped off the plane. The night sky out here was enormous, and the stars shone back much brighter than in the city. Nick could hear the kids bemoaning bedtime, and reluctantly agreeing with their Dad to go and wash up and get ready for bed while their grandmother cleaned up in the kitchen after dinner.

After the initial confusion, which was explained away innocently as them being old friends to Belle's mother-in-law, they ate dinner on the back deck of the property, at the long handmade table with mismatched chairs. He tried his best not to stare, but still was amazed that he was looking at Belle Smith. She looked like a carbon copy of her missing photo, which was everywhere as he grew up, albeit now 20 years older. Considering what she had been through, time seemed to have been kind to her, and she seemed happy and healthy.

He could tell Maz wanted to ask one million questions, just as he did, but they tried their best to make small talk during dinner, while they both stared back into the face of a literal ghost, which had haunted both of their thoughts. One for months and another for the best part of half of their lifetime.

After dinner, Alex stood and wiped his mouth with a cloth that was laid across his lap. Nick had been sizing him up from the minute they had met. He seemed to be a loving and caring husband, and he could see that the property was well run, and the home was beautifully presented. Just how much he knew of Belle's background was a bigger question, and one he hoped he would get answers to.

'Right, I'll get the kids off to bed while you guys have a chat, Mum, you right to wash up?'

His mother smiled back and began to pick up the empty plates around the table. 'Of course, love, it'll be nice to be of use. Britt never lets me lift a finger around here.'

Belle sipped from her wineglass and smiled warmly back at her mother-in-law. 'Maureen, for everything you do for this family, you shouldn't have to do a thing.'

Soon after Maureen had busied herself cleaning up in the kitchen and Alex was in sorting out their boys, Maz moved up to sit beside her and Nick made his way up to sit across from them. Maz took Belle's hand and broke the silence. 'How much do they know?'

'Alex, everything. Maureen, nothing. I've never told a single other person other than my husband.'

'He's been protecting you? All this time?' Nick asked.

'All this time.' She looked inwards to her home at her husband, who was busy chasing one of their sons around the lounge room with a set of pyjamas. 'How did you find me?'

'You changed your licence; we got a hit that it was a fake ID.'

'That was years ago. Why now?'

'New technology. I was tasked with re-investigating your disappearance in Darfield. One of our tech whiz's stumbled across a document that flagged your ID as fake. We never even knew you had a fake ID until a month ago. Anna Denholm told us.'

'Anna.. Wow, how's she doing?'

'Let's get to that later, love,' Maz replied, patting her hand. 'We need to talk about Tom.'

Belle's demeanour completely changed at the sound of his name, and her hand instinctually pulled back. She wrapped both arms around herself and Nick could see herself physically becoming smaller, pulling herself inward and away from danger. 'He's the reason for all of this. He's the reason I'm here.'

'We know. He's dead,' Nick said, matter-of-factly.

Tears welled silently in Belle's eyes, and she lowered her face into her hands and wept. Maz placed her arm around her and hugged her tightly, and she fell in towards her and soon they were both crying. Nick sat a little awkwardly but knew that he was watching a lifetime of fear and anxiety slowly washing away from Belle, and he realised that she was probably for the first time since she was a young girl, feeling like she was free.

When her tears had finally dried, her face took an ugly turn and reddened. 'He raped me. At the lake. My own uncle. Do you have any idea just how scared I was? I was seventeen.'

It all finally made sense. The photos were just the beginning. Tom had taken advantage of his niece, and that was the catalyst for all of this. A scared and lost young girl, who had no one to turn to, who thought the best solution was to just run away from it all.

'I am so, so sorry, Belle. He's gone now, I promise. Just how did you get away? How did nobody notice you?'

She blew her nose and took another sip from her wineglass. 'It was actually a lot easier than I thought it would be. I packed a bag one night, cut all my hair off, and hitched a ride. The first truck I got into took me all the way to Alice. The first few months were the worst. My face was all over the newspapers and TV, and I had to keep my head down. My hair was much shorter, and then I died it black. Eventually, I guess I just started to blend in and forget my past.'

'I know that what he did was the absolute worst thing that anyone could do, Belle, but why didn't you say anything, love? You knew me or even your Mum. You should've spoken up,' Maz said.

She sighed. 'When I think back then now, yes, maybe I should of, but I was terrified. Tom came to me in my room. It was the last time I ever saw him. And told me that if I ever told anyone that he would kill me.'

'So how did you get out here?' he asked.

'I found a job waitressing on the outskirts of Alice after a few months, and the old couple who owned the café let me stay with them. I worked there for two years and one day Alex came in.' Her face lit up at the thought and he could almost see that old smile that had stared back at him through his case file photos.

'It was a quick courtship. He was working on a farm close by and we were married after six months. I moved out here and fell pregnant quickly. I was seven months pregnant when I finally broke. I told him everything.'

He couldn't even imagine how the conversation would've gone back then, Alex and Belle, both young and in love with their whole life ahead of them and Belle drops an absolute bombshell on him, she is Belle Smith, the missing school girl who is on the news and is being spoken about in every café and pub across Australia.

'And how did he take it?'

She laughed again. 'Wasn't much he could do; I was due in a few months. Once the shock wore off, he was amazing. He's protected me all this time. Back when we were younger, there were many times when someone would say to me, gee you look familiar, I can't place you, and he would brush them off and say I was a movie star. I guess it turned into a game for him.'

'It may have been a game for him, but a lot of people were looking for you, Belle, a lot of police resources. Not to mention your own family,' Nick said.

'I know, and for that, I'm truly sorry. I guess there is nothing I can say that can take back what I did, but I am safe here. I am happy. I have a beautiful husband and a beautiful family. My life turned out okay.'

Alex soon joined them, and Belle and Maz caught up on everything that had happened in Darfield over the past 20 years. Belle filled them in on her life on the farm and raising her boys on the remote outback cattle station. Nick watched her and Alex intently and saw a happy and healthy marriage. They were both very much in love with each other still, which wasn't always the case, and although time had aged Belle, things in the end hadn't turned out so badly for her.

Chapter Thirty-Seven

Nick dived into the cool river and kicked his feet hard as he pushed through the water. The undercurrent pushed him ever so slightly to the left, but from years of experience, he had begun his swim at the far-right side of the riverbank where the bush began. He rolled over onto his back and let the current slowly move him towards the sandbar, which after thousands of years and floods and droughts, spread its way nearly to the other side of the river.

He was back in Milford, his hometown, after a whirlwind two weeks. His face was on every newspaper in the nation and he was on every television screen as well. He was due back in the city the next day for an interview with Channel Nine's sixty minutes program and knew that he needed to get packed and prepare for the long drive back to Sydney.

Nick and Maz had flown back to Mildura and decided together to make the drive out to Darfield, and let the Smiths know in person what they had found. It was obviously an incredible shock to the whole family, but when they finally found out the truth, they seemed to understand. Once the news was delivered, Nick stood in the driveway in Belgrove next to the large machinery shed and made the call to his Chief.

'Morning detective, how are you going up there? Any leads so far?'

The trip had been a blur, and he struggled to hold in a wide grin as he dropped the bombshell. 'Morning Chief, I'll do you one better. We found her, alive and well.'

There was a silence on the end of the line for a beat, and he thought he could hear the sound of a hand smacking on the desk. 'You what?! How? Christ mate, great work! Where was she?'

Nick explained to his boss their journey to Tranbie, and about walking straight into Belle, happily married with a family, and her own journey back in the year 2000, to get away from her uncle after what he did to her.

'God, all of this work and time. If she had spoken up, none of this would have happened.'

'Agreed.'

'This is going to be another circus. Where are you now?'

'Back in Darfield, we've just told the Smiths.'

'Okay. Good. I'm going to speak to Elsie in media relations, I'll need you back here by tomorrow, we'll need to do a press conference and I'm sure there'll be journo's knocking down our doors.'

Nick sighed and tried to mentally prepare for the onslaught that he knew was inevitable. He still hadn't quite wrapped his head around the fact that he and Maz had solved one of Australia's most famous missing persons cases. He looked around at the small farm and hoped that there would be some new, happier memories made here in the future. 'I'll see you tomorrow then, Chief.'

Back in Milford, he made his way out of the water and back up the riverbank towards Bec, who was lounging on a towel, engrossed in a book. He sat down beside her and looked back out across the river; the water moved slowly today and even the birds perched in surrounding gumtrees seem to remain quieter than usual. Everyone was at peace here, it seemed, and he wasn't looking forward to leaving so soon and heading back to reality.

His phone rang beside him, and he answered it after the second ring. 'Enjoying your holiday?' Maz said down the line.

'Not long enough sadly, how did it all go? No issues?'

Maz had been in touch with Belle after Vanessa and Arthur had begged for contact information for her, and she had finally rung her mother and father again after a long 23 years for a short conversation. Plans had soon been made and Maz had flown back to the Northern Territory to bring Belle personally home back to Belgrove to see her parents once again. This had all been done in complete secrecy, as half of the nation's media seemed to be permanently entrenched now in Darfield, with any morsel of information from the case still being plastered across televisions as 'Breaking News.'

'Better than I expected. Lots of tears, lots of apologies.'

'I'm glad to hear it.'

'Thanks again, for everything. We wouldn't have found her if it wasn't for you.'

He scoffed. 'Don't sell yourself short, Sergeant. You followed this through to the end and you found her.'

He heard her take a long inhale of her cigarette before she continued, 'So, what's next for you?'

'I'm headed back to Sydney.'

'Well, enjoy your last few hours at home, and safe drive. Say hi to Bec from me.'

'Will do.'

Nick hung up the phone and stretched back out on the towel beside Bec, who now had her novel resting across her face, blocking out the sunlight. 'How's Maz? How'd it go?' she asked.

'It went well. Everyone was happy. And the media didn't sniff it out, so that's probably more important for now. They need time and space.'

'I still can't believe it. I still can't believe you found her.'

'Me either, to be honest. I wasn't expecting a happy ending.'

Bec rolled pulled the book off her face and rolled on her side towards him and offered a smile. 'Shall we pack up? I'm dreading the long drive.'

He looked back out across the river and basked in the peaceful silence. The only noise was the steady buzz of the cicadas and the singing of a nearby magpie. He smiled back at her. 'How about I push this interview, and we stay a little longer?'

THE END

Thank you so much for reading my novel.

If you enjoyed Into The Flames, make sure you check out my debut novel 'Warranilla', which is the first book in this Nick Vada series I have been writing. It's on Amazon Books now.

Also, if you enjoyed my novel, please consider leaving a rating/review on my Amazon book page or on Goodreads. It means a lot to hear what my readers think, as reviews are hard to come by and I personally read every review.

Jason Summers

Printed in Great Britain
by Amazon

44996818R00199